Wild Boy

The Tales of Rowan Hood
By Nancy Springer

Rowan Hood, Outlaw Girl of Sherwood Forest

Lionclaw

Outlaw Princess of Sherwood

Wild Boy

A Tale of Rowan Hood

Nancy Springer

Philomel Books ❦ New York

Library of Congress Cataloging-in-Publication Data
Springer, Nancy. Wild boy, a tale of Rowan Hood / Nancy Springer.
p. cm. Sequel to: Outlaw princess of Sherwood, a tale of Rowan Hood.
Summary: Determined to avenge the death of his swineherd father at the hands of the Sheriff
of Nottingham, Rook finally gets his chance when the Sheriff's son is captured by Robin Hood.
[1. Revenge—Fiction. 2. Fathers and sons—Fiction. 3. Friendship—Fiction. 4. Robin Hood
(Legendary character)—Fiction. 5. Middle Ages—Fiction.] I. Title.
PZ7.S76846Wi 2004   [Fic]—dc22   2003019146   ISBN 0-399-24015-2
1   3   5   7   9   10   8   6   4   2
First Impression

For Jaime

Wild Boy

One

🌿

Flat on his belly on the riverbank, Rook slipped his hands silently into the eddying pool. Here at the curve of the river, fat brown trout would be hiding in the shadow of the overhang. Letting his hands dangle in the icy water, for a timeless time Rook waited, watching and listening. An outlaw in Sherwood Forest could never be heedless of danger. But Rook did not stiffen when he heard branches rattling, the thud of hooves on loam, the creak of saddle leather. He lay alert, yet at ease, waiting for the horseman to ride past. Rook knew that his bare, skinny body lay weather-browned and almost invisible in the bracken, his shaggy black hair at one with the shade of the shaggy willows. This was how he liked to be, like a wild animal of the forest, a hidden, solitary creature who didn't have to care too much, or think, or remember.

His hands swayed with the river currents, seemingly of their own accord drifting deeper beneath the over-hang, waiting for a trout to brush their fingers. In the bracken near Rook's side lay half a dozen silver speck-led fish. Rook wanted to go back to Rowan with enough fat trout to feed her and the others. But it was not that he cared about Rowan, Rook told himself, even though she was Rowan Hood, archer and healer, daughter of a woods witch and Robin Hood himself. Rook kept his distance from her and Beau and Lionel. He did his share, that was all. Rowan brought in small game and healing herbs; Lionel hunted deer. Even Beau, that laughing pest, gathered hazelnuts and such. And Rook caught fish to eat.

Deep in the green-dark pool beneath his fingers, shadows moved. Deep in the oak forest all around him moved shadows of a different sort. It was as if a breeze had stirred the greenshade, nothing more, or as if trout had slipped through deep water. But watching, Rook al-lowed his eyes to widen. Robin Hood's outlaws were on the hunt for something. The horseman? He had passed Rook by, but Rook could still hear the rustling of brush around his horse's flanks.

2

Rook did not move, did not turn his head to look. Let Robin do what he wanted.

Ah, Rook thought. Despite the icy water he felt a whisper of motion: trout fins fanning. Slowly, softly, Rook curled his hand, fingertips tickling the trout's belly. To catch trout this way he had to act as if he loved them. Perhaps he did. Sweetly, sweetly he caressed the fish until it had entirely relaxed into the cup of his hand. Then he whipped it out of the water. A splash, a shining arc, and the trout flopped in the bracken, gills gasping. Rook placed it with the others, barely noticing how his hands had gone numb with cold. A stag or a wild boar or a wolf would not notice the cold. But even a wolf must beware of enemies, Rook knew. Had anyone heard him move, or seen him?

Snap, a branch broke, not far away. Hooves stamped. Twigs rattled.

Flat in the bracken, Rook crawled behind the massive trunk of an ancient willow. Once in its sheltering shadow, he eased his head up, peering toward the commotion.

He saw the horse first, at a distance between oak boles, a great, rampaging black horse seemingly at war with the green clinging forest, kicking and plunging, whacking and hacking worse than a woodcutter with an ax. And the rider's brass helmet and breastplate made a racket like a tinker mending pans. He wore livery that made Rook glower, in the colors of Nottingham, forsooth. It was one of the Sheriff's men, and the fool had ridden his horse into ivy. When would these high-horse braggarts learn? There he struggled, his mighty steed caught in vines as strong as a hangman's noose, and there he could stay.

No, it appeared that his situation would soon become even worse. Rook gave a low growl of pleasure, because now he saw the outlaws, their backs to him and their bows at the ready, waiting for Robin's signal.

It came—a birdlike whistle, mocking and cheery. Within a heartbeat, a dozen outlaws broke cover to confront the rider from all points of the compass, longbows drawn, ringing the man with razor-sharp steel arrow points.

Rook stood and walked forward, silent as always on his bare feet.

Ambushed, the horseback rider startled like a deer. A stray branch caught at his helmet and knocked it off.

The outlaws started to laugh.

From atop the frothing horse, the rider glared around him, his gaze raking the outlaws. Rook saw dark eyes in a thin, pale face dotted with freckles. Narrow shoulders. Arms like sticks, skinny hands trembling on the reins.

"By my troth, it's a boy!" cried a voice Rook knew well. Robin Hood, the outlaw leader, stood with his bow lowered, his golden curls glinting in a shaft of sunlight and his blue eyes sparkling with fun.

Yes, the horseback rider was a boy. A stripling no bigger or older than Rook was.

"What are you doing on that horse, lad?" inquired the tallest outlaw, Little John.

"I know him," said another outlaw. "It's the Sheriff's son."

Rook felt a sudden thicket of emotion clot his chest, passions like thorns, like knives, fit to pierce him from within. His hands clenched into fists.

"The Sheriff's son!" A chorus of mockery burst from the outlaws.

"It's Little Lord Nottingham?"

"Ooooh! On Papa's horse?"

"Watch out, sonny. Papa will spank."

"Papa will be worried if you're not home for supper." Smiling as if he almost meant this, Robin stepped forward and started cutting the ivy away with his long hunting knife.

"Come on," said Little John to the others. Several of

them stepped forward to help. Little John, standing almost seven feet tall, reached up to lift vines away from the rider, but the youngster pulled back from him.

"Get your foul hands off of me!"

The boy should have remained silent. His voice cracked and squeaked. The outlaws laughed anew. Chuckling, Robin joined Little John. "Now, be careful," he told him, owlish. "Do be careful, Little John, lest yon fierce warrior take offense at your foul hands."

"Ay, by my poor old body, we can't have foul hands touching a Nottingham."

The two of them untangled the boy and lifted him off the horse as he thrashed and windmilled and struggled against them. "I do not yield!" he cried. He wore a short sword but did not think to reach for it, just squirmed and flailed like an eel. "Let me go!" he yelled. "You let me go, or my father will kill you all!"

"Spitfire!" Robin exclaimed, grinning, as they laid the boy on the ground and took the sword away. "What are we going to do with him, merry men?"

Outlaws yelled suggestions, some of them more serious than others.

"Dance a reel on him!"

"Give him a shave with a blunt arrowhead."

"Spank him and send him back to his papa."

"Hold him for ransom."

"Hold him hostage."

"Give him a Sherwood Forest welcome."

Then spoke a different voice, a thick panting voice Rook barely recognized as his own, although he felt it bursting like a wild boar out of the sharp, tangled wilderness in his chest. "Kill him."

Robin Hood swung around, crouching to flee or fight, his face a pale, startled oval. The other outlaws snatched at their bows. For a heartbeat there was silence like a scream.

"Rook, lad," Robin said almost in a gasp. "You took us unawares. Put a feather in your cap for that." He stood tall again, and the ruddy color returned to his cheeks. "If you ever wear a cap."

Rook paid Robin no heed. All his thoughts were for the Sheriff's son. He felt the skinny, freckle-faced boy staring up at him from the ground, could almost hear him thinking the scornful thoughts of an aristocrat: *He's filthy, he smells, keep him away from me.* Proud son of Nottingham. "Kill him," Rook repeated, his voice as dark and clotted as the brambles in his heart.

"What, Rook, do you think we'd kill a child? To eat,

perchance?" Robin recovered his grin. "Nay, there'll be a feast in his honor tonight. Tell Rowan and the others, will you?"

Rook said nothing, only glared at the boy on the ground. The boy stared back at him, his narrow face white and hard. A child? Rook himself stood no taller, no older, no stronger, but he knew himself to be no child. He was an outlaw, and like a wolf he could be killed by anyone who cared to carry his severed head to Nottingham for a reward, and like a wolf he would kill. He would kill this freckled, snotty brat if he got a chance.

Two

T̲hat night, fresh ember-baked trout tasted like wood to Rook. Instead of eating, he leaned against the stones that formed a natural wall around the rowan hollow, watching as the others ate. Watching Rowan, who seemed to think always of the others, lay her portion aside to place more wood on the fire. Watching Lionel, the overgrown lummox, gulp his dinner, bones and all. Watching Beau, the newcomer, pick at her food and talk. Beau loved to talk. "*Mon foi,* this is a stout trout," she declared to no one in particular. "A trout *femme, n'est-ce pas?*"

"Only you," complained Lionel, wiping his mouth on his sleeve, "would want to know whether your dinner was a girl trout or a boy trout."

"*Mais quel dommage,* a shame if one cannot tell, *oui?*"

Beau still wore the crimson tunic and yellow leggings of the high king's page boy. Many had not known she was a girl. Soberly Lionel turned her joke against her. "Sometimes people just can't tell, Belle."

Beau straightened, her black eyes flashing. "You no call me Belle!"

"But my dear Belle," protested Lionel with round-eyed gravity, "we know you're not really a boy. Just as your fair tresses are not really yellow." Although Beau's hair still hung golden to her shoulders, its black roots had grown out almost a hand's width. "Fair hair once yellow, Belle, O!" Lionel sang as if he were thinking of composing a ballad.

"No Belle, I tell you!"

"But you are a girl, mademoiselle, and *femme* for *Beau* is *Belle*."

"Bah! Stop it. Sounds like ding-dong."

"Goodness gracious." Lionel's moon face lighted up, his baby blue eyes angelic. "Very well, how is this? You stop talking with that annoying phony Frankish accent, and I'll stop calling you Belle."

"I talk how I like. Go milk yourself."

Sitting quietly in her wilderness hideout with her wolf-dog at her side, Rowan took no part in the bickering, amusement showing only in her warm eyes. In the firelight's tawny glow her grave face seemed to float in the night, spiritous, like the *aelfe,* woodland denizens who were her kin. On one finger she wore the two remaining circlets of the many-stranded ring that had belonged to her half-*aelfin* mother. Lionel wore his strand on a silver chain under his tunic. Beau's strand shone on her hand, greasy from eating fish.

Lionel protested, "But, my dear little Belle—"

"Clodpole, make silent the big mouth or I stuff my fist in it." Tossing a trout head at him, Beau grinned as if it were a treat to be teased. Lionel had always teased Ettarde too, calling her "dear little lady," which she had hated. Ettarde would have laid her fish on a dock leaf, dissected it as if it were a logic problem, then wiped her hands daintily with the kerchief she kept tucked in her sleeve. Remembering Ettarde, Rook reminded himself that he did not miss her, just as he was sure she did not miss his dirty face or his black hair tangled worse than a moorland pony's mane. Even as a runaway, Etty had remained a princess, and Rook detested aristocrats.

But even worse he hated the Sheriff of Nottingham, a commoner who gave himself the airs of an aristocrat.

Rowan glanced at Rook across the rowan hollow and

11

gave him one of her rare smiles. Did she sense his dark thoughts? Perhaps. Rook had been silent tonight, but Rowan knew silence was Rook's custom. He seldom spoke unless it was necessary, and it was not necessary now. He did not have to smile back at her either. Rowan was wise. Rowan knew that a wild boy did not smile.

Consigning Rook's father to die, the Sheriff of Nottingham had smiled.

Rook's hands clenched at the thought. A growl formed deep in his throat. But at that moment Tykell, the wolf-dog, lifted his gray-furred head and growled aloud. Someone was coming.

In one swift motion Rowan stood, arrow-straight in her green kirtle, hearkening. Beau scrambled to ready her new bow and arrows, and even that great slug Lionel alerted, one hand on his quarterstaff. On his feet like Rowan, Rook reached for the dagger he wore at his belt.

Tykell's growl quieted. He wagged his plumy tail.

Within the next eyeblink, without a sound, not even the scrape of a deerskin boot on stone or the rustle of leather against a rowan leaf, Robin Hood slipped over the boulders and leapt lightly down to stand in the hollow.

"Sacre bleu," said Beau, "it's a dastardly scoundrel if I've ever seen one."

Robin kissed Rowan on the side of her head, smoothing her brown hair back from her face. "Daughter," he greeted her. Whatever the business was, Rook knew, Robin could have sent a messenger, but as usual he had come himself for the sake of seeing Rowan. The next moment, his eager blue glance scanned the others. "Scoundrel yourself," he told Beau with a smile. "No mischief for me here? Hast seen aught of the Sheriff's son?"

Lionel and Beau and Rowan exclaimed in unison, "The *Sheriff's son*?"

"Fire-spitting youngling on a horse too big for him." Robin's gaze caught on Rook. "Didn't you tell them?"

Rook only growled, his eyes narrowing to slits.

Rowan answered for him. "Tell us what?"

"Why, you were all invited for dinner, lass, to give the Nottingham lad a Sherwood Forest welcome." Robin's eyes glinted with fun as he turned toward Lionel. "We traded the horse for a goatskin full of milk and a whole wheel of yellow cheese—"

"Cheese?" Lionel yelped, lurching to his enormous feet.

"—and a dozen loaves of white wheat bread."

"And *bread*?"

"But it doesn't matter," Robin went on, "because the imp has given us the slip." Robin said this with a certain admiration. "First he refused to tell us his name, then he cursed my ancestry and threatened that his father would hang us by our heels from our own oak tree, and then while we passed the mead around, somehow he befooled us all."

"*Mon foi,* he got away? From *you*?" Beau's dark eyes sparkled with mockery to remind Robin that she herself had once gotten away from him and his merry men.

But Robin seemed not to mind. "He got away clean as a whistle."

"You hadn't tied him up?" Rowan asked, soberly teasing.

"Why, no, lass, he's just a bit of a boy."

Bit of a boy? Rook felt emotions like blackthorn bristle in his chest. He felt himself starting to tremble with rage. But no one seemed to notice.

Serious now, Rowan thought aloud. "He'll bring Nottingham down on you like a hornet's nest."

"If he can find his way home! But I'm more afraid he'll come to harm." Robin's hands flew up like startled doves. "He's afoot, he has no idea where he is, and how will he fend for himself in the woods? He's likely to starve—"

"Let him starve!" Rook burst out, fists clenched like his heart.

Every head turned; every face stared at him. "Goodness gracious," Lionel said.

Robin asked Rook, "Lad, what has the Sheriff's son ever done to—"

"He's devil get!" Rook matched Robin Hood stare for stare.

But he felt Rowan's gaze on him. She said slowly, "Rook, I've often known you to speak good sense, and I've never known you to waste breath in anger."

He turned his head to face her, but said nothing. His reasons for hatred were his own.

With a low, worried note in his voice, Robin asked, "Rowan, lass, what if the lad comes here? I was hoping he might see the light of your fire. . . ."

"He'll come to no harm here."

She spoke firmly, as was her right. She was the healer, and her spirit inhabited this rowan hollow; nothing evil could happen here. Still, she looked to Rook for his promise.

Rook nodded to her. He, too, wore one strand of Rowan's silver ring on a leather thong slung around his neck, so that the circlet rested over his heart. Until he gave it back, he was a member of Rowan's band.

But it was not for her to say whether the Sheriff's son would come to harm on the tors where Rook denned like a fox in a cave. Rook met Rowan's gaze for only a moment more before he turned and strode away, his bare, hard feet carrying him surely into the night on his own.

Three

At daybreak, Rook sat cross-legged on a crag near the top of a steep, rocky tor. He had not slept much, but then, wild things seldom did. From his rocky vantage, he watched Sherwood Forest awakening like a living being, breathing its morning mist, steam rising white between the deeply green oaks as they stretched their limbs toward the sun. But no sunshine would caress them today. The sky brooded leaden gray and low, heavy with rain.

Rook noticed that Rowan and Beau and Lionel were up already, even before the thrushes and wood larks. He could not see them through the lush leaves of early summer, but he saw hints, movements. And he saw other such intimations throughout Sherwood Forest, shadows flitting beneath the trees, thickets stirring even though no breeze blew. Those shadows and stirrings were Robin Hood's outlaws on the hunt. Evidently the Sheriff's son had not yet been found.

Let him be lost. Let him starve and die.

As if she heard him thinking, Rowan slipped into view through the feathery foliage of the rowan grove. In her oak-green kirtle, with her dark hair pulled back in a braid, she did not so much walk into sight as appear like a spirit of the forest, soundless in her soft deerskin boots, her bow and arrows riding like wings on her back. She looked up at Rook, and although she was too far away for him to see her warm glance of greeting, he felt it. Then she looked downward at her footing and started climbing the rocky slope toward him. *Too slowly,* Rook thought. *If only she could heal herself.* He could see that Rowan's legs, broken in a man trap the autumn before, still troubled her. There was no telling whether she would ever be strong again.

Rook sighed, slipped off his rock and walked down the tor to meet her, digging his callused heels into the rocky slope.

"We're going to help search for the boy, Rook," she told him as soon as she was close enough to speak to him without shouting.

"Not I."

She nodded in acknowledgment. Rowan never gave orders; she considered herself a strand of the band, not its leader. But her gentle brown gaze studied Rook. "What is wrong?" she asked.

"Nothing your touch can cure." With his lips tightened into a line like a flint knife's edge, Rook turned away.

And started walking.

Homeward.

Although not even to himself did Rook admit where he was going.

As quiet as a brown owl feather, Rook slipped through the forest, edging his way between rocky scarps and great grandfather oaks and thickets as thorny as the bitter tangle in his heart. His meandering way followed no path. Only instinct led him back, back to—

No. He would not think about that life. Or the day it had ended.

But whatever he tried not to think, his wayward footsteps carried him toward the farthest edge of the forest, toward a straggle of woods where he had not ventured since—

Since that day. A dank day, like this one—Rook scorned the damp air chilling his bare shoulders. A wild thing does not feel cold. He blinked his eyes and shook his head, trying to shake away the memory of what had happened that day a year and a half ago, the day he had become an outlaw, hunted for bounty, like a wolf.

Very well. A wolf does not cry.

Now there was a path, veering down a steep hillside, probably made by deer and less fortunate wanderers going down to water. Rook seldom allowed himself to feel thirst, but knew he should drink once a day or so to stay alive. This might be as good a chance as any. He turned the downhill way and ghosted along to one side of the path— outlaws knew better than to follow trails.

There. His guess had been right. He could hear the soft voice of living water murmuring ahead.

At the bottom of a rocky gorge, swift water leapt and ran like a flood of black squirrels. It was a fine, full, rushing stream, good for trout's long-finned larger cousin, the grayling. The scent and sight of such water made Rook's chest swell, as always. Halfway down the side of the gorge he stood for a moment just looking—

"Rook."

The low voice jabbed him like a spear point. He

jumped, turned and looked straight into the eyes of the Sheriff's son.

And the brat remembered his name.

Huddled against the damp belly of a boulder, the boy gazed back at Rook, his dark eyes like a shot deer's. His pale, narrow face glistened with moisture; his hunched shoulders trembled. Then Rook saw dark blotches on his jerkin and leggings: blood. Just below the boy's right knee, half hidden by dried leaves, clung a great cold arc of steel.

Man trap.

Those heavy saw-toothed jaws were built to harm as well as to hold. The boy's leg was broken. Not just broken. Mangled.

Crouching, growling, Rook backed away. There in the trap the Sheriff's son could very well stay. It was as if fate had put him there. It was justice.

"Rook," said the Sheriff's son in the same low, level tone, "help me."

"My curse on you," Rook told him, thorns in his voice. "Die there."

"Why do you hate me?"

Silence. Rook felt the boy's gaze on him. He felt the

stricken, trembling pain in that gaze, but even more, he felt how much the Sheriff's son was not saying. The proud brat had not screamed for help. He did not beg. He did not speak again. He waited for an answer.

In that silence Rook heard his own father's scream.

He clenched his fists until his ragged fingernails bit into the palms of his hands. "Devil's son! My father died in a man trap because of yours."

"Then your father was a lawbreaker."

"He was not! He was a brave man and an honest one." Passion made Rook clumsy. He stumbled to his knees amid rocks and loam, panting, his chest tight with the pain of remembering his father. "He was . . . a swineherd. . . ." Dull, dirt-ridden word, it did not begin to tell what Rook's father had been. Jack-o-Shoats, Jack Pigkeep, Jack By-the-Woods, none of his names bespoke the swineherd's courage. Rook's father had lived on his own, outside the village, far from the lord's protection and tyranny, near the forest's edge. Without the help of neighbors, he had fought off wolves and human marauders trying to steal his pigs. And he had raised his motherless son. *Kept me. Took care of me. Fed me.* And fed others. Peasants would have starved during the long winters without the smoked meat Jack Woodsby had provided. Scars had whitened every part of Jack Woodsby's body from the tusks of wild swine. Every spring Jack the swineherd had risked his life, capturing the young wild pigs. Had the Sheriff's son ever faced the charge of a wild boar? Rook wondered. Most likely not. Most likely the snot-nosed boy had never even seen a dark, swift, prick-eared long-legged smart-eyed sharp-snouted contrary-minded scourge of a hog such as the ones his father had pastured through the summer and herded into the forest in the fall—

Which was when it had happened.

Between clenched teeth Rook told the Sheriff's son, "My father brought hogs here to the woods to fatten. . . ." Rook struggled to speak, remembering that deadly day. He had been up in a beech tree, shaking the boughs to send down beechnuts for the pigs to eat along with mushrooms and the roots they grubbed from the ground. His father had heard a shoat choking on an acorn and had run into the bushes after it.

Then—the scream. His father's scream.

Rook whispered, "He stepped into one of those accursed man traps."

White-faced and shaking, the boy appeared to be learning what it meant to be caught in a man trap. The king's foresters had set this one where the trail narrowed, passing between a tree trunk and the boulder, where the leaves that hid the steel would naturally gather. They would not be back to check their handiwork for another month or two, hoping to find the moldering skeleton of an outlaw, or any poor man who had dared to venture into the king's hunting lands. Already the Sheriff's son listened silently, lacking strength to talk. Soon he would faint. He might well die of his injury before thirst and starvation took him. The horrible hurt of the thing, that was how . . . how Jack By-the-Woods had died.

My father.

The Sheriff's son met Rook's stare without blinking, silent.

Rook's mouth worked hard to shape the words. "I couldn't get him out." It took two strong yeomen to spring a man trap. "I ran. . . ." Rook struggled to speak, remembering his father's shriek of pain, his father's stricken face. "I ran all the way to Nottingham for help, but no one . . ." Cowards, they had been afraid. "They told me to go to your father."

The Sheriff's son whispered, "My father is duty sworn to uphold the laws of the king."

"Swineherds roamed these woods before the king was thought of! I knelt to your father. I *knelt*." As he was kneeling right now in the dirt and leaf loam. "I begged him." Rook trembled now like the Sheriff's son, but not with pain; he shook with rage. "I begged him to spare my father's life."

"My father would not refuse such a plea," said the Sheriff's son.

Rook's voice fought its way out through fury fit to choke him. "He did refuse. He said, 'Bad cess to you, what's one stinking swineherd the less? Let him die.'"

"You lie!" The boy pushed himself upright, wrath giving him strength, although his face paled whiter than ever. "My father never said so. You are a liar!"

Watching the boy's anger, Rook became suddenly very calm. "Meseems your *father* must be a liar," he said.

"Not so! He will punish you for saying so."

"I have already cursed him to his face and he has made me an outlaw for it." *As if watching my father die weren't bad enough?* Rook burst into dark laughter. Dark and cruel. His father had taught him no cruelty—even when slaughtering his hogs, Jack Woodsby had struck quick and true so as not to be cruel—but Rook considered that he had learned cruelty from the Sheriff of Nottingham. Rook smiled.

"Tell me that your father is a liar and a scurvy knave," he said, "and I will help you."

"Knave yourself!" the Sheriff's son flared, panting with pain.

"I mean it," said Rook, no longer shaking, sitting back now with his hands around his bare brown knees, quite cool. "Tell me that your father is a black-hearted villain, and I will set you free."

The Sheriff's son gazed back at him, cold sweat standing like dew on his wincing eyelids, his trembling lips.

"Tell me that your father is a clodpole and a scoundrel," Rook urged, "or words of your own choosing. Say it."

But the boy slumped against the boulder as if all his strength were gone. He turned his face to the stone.

Quietly he said, "No."

Rook stood up to walk away. "Then stay where you are and die."

Four

The boy lay with his eyes closed, with the side of his face pressed against cold stone. Rook tried to turn away, but something stirred in him like breath of the forest in the limbs of the trees, a wild sigh of second thought. He looked again at the Sheriff's son, and saw tears trembling at the corners of the boy's clenched eyes.

Yet the Sheriff's son would not betray his father.

Rook's heart turned over. He knew what it was to love a father.

And to be loyal to him. Lady have mercy, but the Sheriff's son was brave.

Leave him. Let him starve.

But already Rook knew he couldn't do it. His father's

life and death had taught Rook what he could and couldn't do. There had been a time, as he had sat beside his father toward the end, that his father had gone mad with the pain and begged him to take the hog-sticking knife and kill him.

Rook hadn't been able to do it.

He let out a long, shaky breath and swallowed hard. He muttered, "A pox on all that comes out of Nottingham." Then he lifted his head, put his fingers to his teeth and whistled. His alarm signal rose wavering at first, then high and clear, as shrill as a hawk's scream.

He heard a gasp, and looked down to see that the Sheriff's son had fainted. In a moment, cold rain began to fall.

It took a long time for help to arrive. Rook sat in the rain by the boy's side, waiting. He had to whistle twice more before he heard the faint answer of Robin Hood's horn. One of Robin's men found them finally, and slipped off his jerkin to lay it over the unconscious, rain-drenched boy. Rook wore no jerkin nor even leggings, just a wrapping around his waist and breech. He scorned to shiver. A stag or fox or badger does not feel the cold. Neither should a wild boy, creature of the forest.

Silently Rook took his place on the opposite side of the man trap from the outlaw, but even though they leaned on its stubborn springs with all their combined strength, it would not open. They bore down on it, straining till they shook.

"Wait," said a quiet voice, and Rook looked up to see Rowan limping toward him along the ravine, with Tykell running puppyish circles around her. The wolf-dog bounded up to the Sheriff's son, sniffed his unconscious head, then charged off toward the rowan hollow. Rowan stood looking at the boy in the man trap, her thin face taut. She had to be remembering how it had felt, the steel jaws springing shut, both her legs snapping like saplings.

Rowan said, "He's likely to bleed to death if you open that. We need to have bandaging at the ready." Placing her bow and arrows to one side, she drew her dagger and began to rip at the hem of her kirtle. "Lady have mercy, he's pale." Stilling her knife a moment, she knelt beside the Sheriff's son, feeling his hand, his forehead. "And *cold*."

Rook scowled, watching: Rowan cared too much.

How could she care so much for a boy she didn't even know? The look on her face made Rook blurt at her roughly, "He won't die!"

She gave him a quizzical glance, and he remembered that he had wanted the Sheriff's son to die. But Rowan said only, "We need to get him to shelter. Toads take it, where is everyone?"

In the distance, Tykell barked. A moment later, a single pebble rattled down the slope, and there stood Robin Hood, rain flattening his blond curls darkly against his head. "By my troth," Robin murmured, "caught in one of his own father's traps."

But there was no gloating in Robin's tone.

Rook heard brush crash at the top of the ravine and turned to look up there, knowing it had to be that clumsy newcomer, Beau, or perhaps Lionel—although Lionel's big feet were getting better at finding their way quietly around the forest. Hah, it was both of them, led by Tykell. Beau plunged recklessly down the side of the ravine, her parti-colored black-and-golden hair flying. Lionel followed more slowly, stooping from his great height to pass under branches. Even Little John was not so tall and strong as Lionel.

As soon as they saw the boy in the man trap, both of them stopped short. Lionel gasped, his round face as white as a moon. Beau opened her mouth, but for once no words came.

"Lionel, lad, come help here." Robin knelt by the man trap.

The Sheriff's son moaned, stirred, and opened his eyes to look Robin straight in the face. "My father will kill you," he panted.

"Mayhap and perchance," Robin agreed with a gentle nod. "Let's get you out of here, lad." Robin beckoned Lionel to the other side of the trap. Looking at Lionel's full-moon face, Rook saw bad memories shining plainly there.

"My father will find me," the Sheriff's son told Robin. "He will come and save me and kill all of you."

"Quite so. Certainly," said Robin kindly. "We're going to spring it now, lad. It'll hurt."

Rook hoped the brat would scream. No, he hoped he wouldn't. . . . He wanted to watch in scorn, but found that he had to turn his face away. Heard a gasp, but curse the boy, he *was* brave. The trap made more noise, squealing as it opened, than he did. It screeched, reluctant to release its prey, and then Rook heard rather than saw how Beau and the others lifted the boy out of the trap and laid him on the ground. Then the trap closed with a clang. Robin and Lionel had let it spring shut so it would harm no one else, but the very sound hurt Rook. He winced.

After that, he could look. Rowan knelt by the boy, busy with bandages, stanching his bleeding. "What's your name?" she asked him.

Panting, he told her what he had refused to tell Robin. "It's—it's Tod."

"Tod." Robin Hood stooped to lay his mantle over the boy. "It's a good name for you. You're a proper young fox, giving us the slip."

"My curse on you," the boy whispered.

"Young spitfire, you're welcome to curse all you like. How bad is it, Rowan, lass?"

Her careful fingers traced the line of the boy's leg. Gentle, she was so gentle, yet Tod gave a choked cry and fainted again.

Rowan said, "It's a clean break."

"Shall we set it now? Get it over with?"

She shook her head. "His pulse . . . he's too weak. Too cold from this rain. He needs shelter. A fire."

"Carry him to the oak?" Robin's great, hollow oak provided the nearest thing to a roof in Sherwood Forest.

"Too far." Deep in the back of Rowan's level voice Rook heard a quiver of fear. He stared at the boy's face, wet with rain and maybe tears, death white.

"Where, then?"

Rowan bit her lip, and Rook could guess her thoughts. There was the rowan hollow, but the rain poured there the same as anywhere else. There were the tors, with their shallow caves, but they stood steep, forbidding, and too far away from this woodland. This stand of trees, Rook knew, straggled at the very farthest outskirts of Sherwood Forest. Beyond it lay only wasteland, rocky meadow where furze and nettles grew, where goose girls jostled with goatherds and shepherds, cowherds and drovers and swineherds for pasturage of a sort. Where no folk dwelt except—

Rook heard his own throat make a kind of whimper. Every head swung to look at him. Except the boy's. Tod lay as motionless as if he were already dead.

Rook tightened his lips, then growled, "Bring him. Follow me." Turning sharply away from them, he trotted off toward the edge of the woods.

Five

He had not been back there since. Had stayed far away. Had faced the sight of flies emptying his father's dead eyes, but he had not been able to face that other emptiness.

Till now.

With his hard back daring the others to question his leadership, Rook led them through the fringes of the forest, loping between scattered groves and thinning woods onto rocky waste amid clumps of gorse. Only once did he glance behind him. Rowan trotted close by, with the others following. Beau blundered along by Robin Hood's side, still without speaking. Lionel walked, his strides so long he did not have to run to keep up. With no more difficulty than if he had been cradling a baby, he carried the Sheriff's son in his arms.

"Not far." Rook flung the words over his shoulder at Rowan even though he saw no doubt in her rain-streaked face. It was he who doubted. As recently as today's dawn he had known how to feel, whom to hate. But now—what was this sour porridge of emotions in him, making him feel half sick? He ran across a meadow so familiar from another life that it felt stranger than a dream, and his head swam.

And there, sheltering beneath a crooked crab-apple tree, almost as solid as a father it stood.

"A hut!" Rowan murmured.

His old home. Empty.

Solid, because Father had built it out of the stones of the waste, corbeling them inward one on top of the other in a dome shaped like a beehive to form both walls and roof of stone, with a hole at the top for the smoke to go out and daylight to come in. A sturdy, well-built hut, yet it stood abandoned, as Rook had known it would. No one wanted to chance living here, for Jack Swineherd had died a foul death, and evil men had thrown his bones somewhere unburied. Surely he had left behind a restless, angry spirit.

Rook considered, as he stopped beside the hut's low doorway, whether something of his father lingered here. The thought added itself to the emotions churning in him. He did not know whether to hope he might meet with his father's ghost, or fear it.

"A fine hut," said Robin Hood with a quiet, questioning glance.

Rook offered no explanation, just dropped to his hands and knees to crawl through the doorway's stone arch, slipping into the hut like a fox into its den. Inside, his father had dug away the ground to make a hollow almost three feet deep, and because the hut stood atop a well-drained upland, worms and water did not gather there. Large enough for a man to lie down in, the hollow also made the hut tall enough for a man to stand up in, and no commoner could ask for more. A lord in his drafty castle could not lie so snug as a swineherd in this hut.

It took Rook's eyes a moment to comprehend the dimness within, but his hands rested on sheepskin beds, and he knew at once that all was well. Nothing had been touched except by mice and such.

Someone crawled in beside him—Rowan. She turned to crouch at the doorway, and two pairs of hands passed the Sheriff's son in to her headfirst. She cradled the boy under his shoulders and eased him to the sunken floor, shifting him to one side so that rain would not find him through the smoke hole. "He's barely breathing," she said, her voice stretched to a taut whisper. "He needs warmth."

Rook had already found kindling in the accustomed place. Squatting like a squirrel, he arranged straw and twigs in the circle of fire stones, then reached for a rock that jutted to form a shelf—yes, flint and steel still lay there. Rook took one in each hand and struck them together shrewdly, raining a shower of sparks on the dry tinder.

A few sparks caught. Rook saw smoke, then a glow as feeble as the hurt boy's pulse. Blowing on it would be too much, would put it out. Rook fanned it with his hand and gave a gruff call to a pair of enormous feet standing outside the doorway. "Lionel, bring firewood."

"Firewood? But my dear little lad, it's all soaking wet." Lionel's tone revealed how much he detested being wet. "Might I remind you it's raining hard out here—"

"Pigsty," Rook said.

"I am not a pigsty! *You're* the dirty one."

Beau broke her unnatural silence. "*Mon Dieu,* Rook, what you talk about?"

"Pigsty?" came Robin Hood's cheery question. "Where—oh! I see it! In the copse."

"That other hut?" Beau asked. Footsteps moved toward where the pigsty hid amid trees, a beehive-shaped stone shelter just like this one, except with a larger entry and no smoke hole. With fodder stored overhead instead. Rook hoped the others would find some fuel in there. Dry sticks left from leafy branches once put in there for fodder and bedding, perhaps. Or the wood of the fodder shelf itself.

Orange light made Rook blink as his fire put out tiny flames. He fed it kindling a little at a time until it blazed more strongly and he felt its warmth on his wet skin. Only when he felt sure the fire would not go out did he look at the Sheriff's son.

Gray eyes looked back at him. The boy lay conscious, watching him with a quiet, wary stare, like a fox cub. By the boy's side sat Rowan, cradling his broken leg in her healing hands. She could not make it mend, Rook knew, but her touch eased the pain.

"What now?" Rook asked her.

Before she could answer, there was a slight scraping noise. A bundle of firewood landed beside Rook, and then Robin Hood slipped in to bend over the Sheriff's son, his broad shoulders crowding the hut to its limit. "Better, lad?" he asked.

"Go suck eggs."

Defiant, even now? The boy had to have heard the

scare stories folk told of outlaws. How they would steal children from cottages, roast them over flaming bonfires and eat them.

"I'm not afraid of you," the boy said, his voice as thin as straw and not much stronger.

"Good, lad."

"We ought to get the wet clothes off him," Rowan said.

They maneuvered around one another in the confines of the hut, Rowan steadying Tod's leg and Rook edging out of the way as Robin bent over the hurt boy. But when Robin reached to pull off Tod's soaked jerkin, the boy clamped his skinny arms across his chest. "Don't."

"Just trying to help you"—Robin lifted Tod's arms with one hand and tugged the jerkin off with the other—"get dry and warm—"

Robin faltered to silence, staring at the boy's thin body. Even in the dim orange firelight, Rook could see also: Tod's narrow shoulders were striped with welts, his bony ribs mottled with fresh dark bruises.

Between clenched teeth Robin breathed, "Who has done this to you?"

Tod said nothing.

"Your father?"

"He—he beats me only to toughen me."

The look on Robin's face made Rook grab one of the sheepskins and cover Tod with it, not so much for warmth as to hide the marks.

Robin said, "That makes as much sense as stripping the bark off a young tree. To toughen it."

"Father, hush," Rowan said.

Tod's eyes widened and shifted to stare at her.

Not hushed at all, Robin demanded, "Does he beat your mother as well? To toughen her?"

"*Father.* Either be quiet and help me set his leg, or go away." Rowan spoke with the authority of a healer. Robin Hood set his lips in a line like a bowstring and said nothing more.

"Rook," Rowan said, "come here. Help us."

Rook found himself holding the Sheriff's son down while Rowan and Robin peeled the bloody wrappings away from the boy's mangled leg. Knees on Tod's shoulders, hands leaning on his arms to restrain him, Rook felt him shaking. It should have been a pleasure to watch a Nottingham suffer, but Rook felt far away, and staring into Tod's upside-down face made everything seem like a bad dream. Rook heard his own hoarse voice as if it belonged to a stranger. "He's biting his lip."

Blood stood on the boy's mouth and chin. Robin

looked, then without a word he undid his hunting knife from his belt and placed it, tough leather sheath and all, between the boy's teeth.

"We'll set it as quickly as we can," Rowan told Tod. Her shadowy gaze shifted to her father. "Ready? Take hold."

The Sheriff's son was brave, Rook knew by now, but brave can do only so much. Tod arched his back, straining, writhing. He screamed—by all the world's suffering, how he screamed—then went limp. Rook closed his eyes.

"Thank the Lady he fainted," Rowan murmured.

She and Robin were binding the splints on. Rook lunged for the doorway, scrambled out and ran in the pouring rain toward the forest. He barely noticed Lionel and Beau calling to him from the shelter of the pigsty. And he had not yet reached the forest before he fell to his knees and vomited. Although there was not much in him to vomit. He had not eaten.

The rain cooled the boiling porridge of emotions in him somewhat. He turned his face to the sky, let the rain wash his mouth, spat, then got up and started walking toward another place he remembered as if from another life.

Six

It took him several days. First he had to find a young tree, not too thick, with two sturdy branches jutting about at the level of his shoulders. Then he had to cut it and trim it into a shape like a slender cross, after which he had to sharpen the upper end into a rude spear. He carried this weapon at the ready as he stalked toward the place he remembered.

Perhaps he should have told Rowan he would be away for a while. . . . But no, foxes and deer did not need to seek anyone's blessing or say-so. Wolves roamed at will. And so would he.

Slipping through the tangled shadows of Sherwood Forest, Rook expected to meet swarms of Nottingham's men-at-arms in search of the Sheriff's missing son. But in fact he saw only one bored patrol riding through a beech glade.

Other than that, he encountered the usual presences in the forest: frightened peasants poaching firewood or meat, nervous travelers, knights errant and wandering friars, the king's foresters, bounty hunters, Robin Hood's merry men, and other outlaws not nearly so merry or kind. Rook knew when any of these folk were near, but few if any of them were aware of the wild boy.

Rook ate what little he could find as he traveled, only enough to stay alive. Mushrooms. Bilberries. Little bony fish that tasted muddy: dace, chub, perch. Still, eating took time, sleeping took time, stalking and walking took time, days of sunshine then cloud again and rain and then more sun.

He found the wallows at last by the prints of many two-pointed hooves leading there. Rain had freshened the mud, and now a warm afternoon sun glowed down between trees busy growing roots and nuts and acorns for pigs to eat. It was a fine, fine day to be a wild hog. Standing behind a mighty oak with roots dug bare by pig snouts, Rook scanned the sows and shoats lying in the wallows with their long legs and their pointed heads stretched out, mud crusting their dark bristles, many of them asleep. If Rook wanted to take a treat of meat back to Rowan, all he had to do was sneak up and grab a young pig. Getting covered with mud was a small price to pay for roast suckling pork.

But it wasn't hunger for meat that had sent him here. It was a different hunger. An aching hunger the Sheriff's son had put into him, making him burn and churn with hate and love, vengeance against Nottingham, longing for a . . . a dead swineherd.

Year after year Father had come here to capture the young wild pigs for fattening, taking the dog—Rook blinked in surprise at himself, that he had almost forgotten the brindle dog. It had been a companion, a playmate of sorts, and it had helped to keep the wild boars at bay in the spring and herd the shoats in the fall. But the king's foresters had come and cut off some of its toes, laming it so that it couldn't chase deer. One day the dog had not come home. Maybe they had killed it outright.

Maybe it had been caught in a man trap.

Like Father.

Remembering Father was thorny hard and hurtful, but looking at the sleeping pigs eased Rook's tangled feelings somewhat. Just standing in this place gave him some small peace. He began to notice birdsong, felt liquid notes cleansing him, a rainbow shower amid sunshine. Breathing deeply of the moist mud-scented air, he seemed to take in something of his father's spirit, something quiet, brown, accepting . . .

No. He would never accept.

Confound the Sheriff's son. Hand of justice put him in the trap for me; why did I let him live? What is wrong with me? Am I a coward? Am I—

"*Mes yeux,* Rook," said a voice behind him, "why you run away?"

He jerked around. There stood Beau, her grin flashing white, her hair hanging like a black-and-yellow flag. He had been forgetting to listen for danger, he had not heard her approaching, and now—

Pigs screeched and scrambled up, startled by Beau's voice. Mud flew as sows and shoats darted in all directions like a sudden ambush, all the king's men shooting all the king's arrows—but these were arrows bigger than Rook and Beau put together. And with a scream more like a roar, something massive and dark thundered toward Beau.

There was no time to think. Rook reacted, leaping to shield Beau, spear pointed toward the danger, even before he fully comprehended the charging boar, before he really saw the black bristles standing on the razor neck and back, the frothy flash of tusks that could tear him wide open, the crescent red raging eyes. The wild boar hit his spear tip at full speed, its hurtling weight staggering him back, back—but as Rook fell, somehow he remembered to plant the butt of the spear in the earth, and he threw himself on it to keep it there, to keep a few feet of spear between him and death. Only the crossbar stopped the boar from charging right up the length of the spear to slash and trample him.

The boar roared, swerved, sidestepped, still trying to get at Rook even though there was a foot of sharpened wood inside him. The spear must not have pierced his heart, and its green wood couldn't stand up to the boar's strength for long; it would break. Rook's pulse roared in his ears, the boar screamed like an evil spirit, everything was screaming, echoes between the trees, piglets, Rook's muscles, his panting throat—and Beau, screaming as she leapt at the raging boar, dagger in hand. The boar swung its head to slash at her. She sprang aside just in time and leapt like a squirrel onto the boar's back, where its tusks could not reach her. Gripping with her knees, she rode its bruising backbone as it plunged worse than a bucking pony. The dagger flashed in air—a bright steel knife with a filigree hand guard, a weapon worthy of the high king's page boy. The dagger plunged, lifted, plunged again.

The boar did not seem to mind being stabbed at all, but the sudden weight on his back maddened him. He writhed, squalled, bent double trying to slash Beau, reared so that Rook caught a glimpse of his heaving hairy belly. But Rook leapt up with him, hanging on to the butt of the spear. His only chance was to keep hold of it. He saw Beau still on the boar with her knees clamped behind its shoulders and one hand clinging to an ear as she stretched forward with the other, trying to slash the beast's throat.

"Eye!" Rook yelled, panting so that he could barely get the word out. "Stab—eye!" Beau's dagger was not long enough to kill the boar unless she struck through its eye straight into its brain.

She heard him, and she tried. But it was like trying to stab a sixpence hung by a string in a high wind. Her dagger struck cheekbone, then air, then—

Then the spear snapped, and Rook fell, knowing it was over. A huge weight struck him. And then there was only blackness.

He awoke sputtering amid a wet, cold stream landing on his forehead. Blurrily he could see Beau's narrow, elegant face looking down as she poured the contents of her water flask on him.

"Stop it," he said.

"*Sacre bleu,* but someone must wash you once in the blue moon," she said, turning the flask upright but scrubbing at his cheek with her other hand. "It was the luck most fortunate, *non,* that I came when I did?"

The idiot. If she hadn't alarmed the swine with her noise, the boar wouldn't have charged in the first place—but then Rook saw the black glint in her eyes. The rascal, she was teasing him. He scowled and tried to sit up, but felt a great weight lying on his belly and legs. Glancing down, he saw the wild boar, stone dead, lying atop him with Beau's dagger jutting from its eye. Feeling sick, he quickly looked away.

"The *bete gross odieux,* it would have killed you were it not for *moi,*" Beau declared.

Equally true, the boar would have killed her if it were not for him. But Rook only growled, "What are you doing here?"

"*Mon foi,* looking for you! Rowan could not do it. She must nurse Tod—"

Tod, it was now. Not "the Sheriff's son." Tod, as if the snot brat were another member of the band.

"—and Lionel must hunt the meat, so it is for me to

see where you so long go. Are your legs broken?" Beau added hopefully.

Rook didn't think so. He heard a pained and panicky squealing noise, but although it matched his mood, it wasn't coming from him. Also, he would have noticed by now if any part of him hurt enough to be broken. Giving Beau only a glare for reply, he said, "Get the brute off me."

"*Mais certainement*. With my bare hands I will lift it instantly." But already she had turned her pale Grecian profile and was jabbing the shaft of his broken spear under the hog, levering it up. Then she kicked a stone under it, found another stick to prop with, and levered it again. It took quite a bit of this before Rook was able to squirm out from under the wild boar's heavy carcass. Beau offered him a hand to help him up, but he turned his back, scrambled to his feet and looked around. Something was still squealing like a frantic baby.

"Your head's bleeding," Beau said.

Rook could feel it. The back of his head seemed to be the only part of him that seriously hurt. It must have hit a rock as the boar slammed him to the ground. Unsteady on his feet, he trudged toward the wallows, now empty of all swine but one. A runty piglet still struggled in the mud. Not big and strong enough to get out by itself, left behind, it squalled for its mother, cried almost as if it knew Rook had just killed its father. Squealing, it thrashed its short legs in the mud, trying to flee, but Rook slogged over to it and picked it up, slippery little yammering thing. He had to cradle it against his chest with both arms to keep it from squirming away from him. Dizzy, hugging the piglet, he slopped back to Beau, mud dripping in globs off his arms and legs and chest.

"Lovely," Beau declared, staring at him. "What we need that for? *Beaucoup* meat we have already." With a languid gesture she indicated the boar's hefty carcass.

Rook did not answer her. He said only, "Give me your tunic string."

She stared at him, then at the long crimson lacing that closed her crimson tunic, then back at him again.

"I'm not going to look at you!" Rook restrained himself from reminding Beau that her chest was as flat as his own. "I need a string."

She muttered, *"Sacre bleu,"* but untied the lacing, pulled it free of her tunic and handed it to him. Rook tied one end of the string around his piglet's hind leg above the hock.

"You're welcome," Beau said.

Ignoring the hint for thanks, Rook set the piglet on the ground and secured the other end of the lacing to a sapling. The piglet strained against the tether and squealed, but Rook gentled its muddy head with his muddy hand. "Hush," he told it. He pulled a packet of cold cooked perch from his belt and gave it to the piglet. The little animal gulped the fish, dock leaves and all.

"Mon foi," said Beau.

"He's a runkling," Rook growled. "A runt. He'll die if someone doesn't take care of him."

Not looking at Beau, he watched the piglet eat.

"My father used to call me Runkling," he said.

Seven

A baby *pig?*" exclaimed a boyish voice from the shadows of a hemlock grove.

"A *pet* pig, forsooth," declared someone else in more manly tones.

"Walking on a leash, by my poor old eyes!"

Rook recognized the third, quizzical voice as Robin Hood's. Robin always thought he knew everything, but Runkling wasn't walking on a leash at all. Actually the shoat scurried ahead of Rook as he pretended to pull back on the string tied to its hind hock. The pig went where he wanted because it thought it was getting away from him. Such was the contrary nature of swine.

Rook wanted to tell Robin he was wrong, but he couldn't seem to get his mouth open and say the words. Too tired. Too worn out to do anything except keep stumbling after Runkling and Beau. But why so weary? It had taken only two days for Beau to lead him to this new hideout of Robin's, and there had been plenty of boar meat to eat. Why, Rook wondered hazily, did he feel so weak that he was staggering?

"Phew, it stinks," said the first voice, the high-pitched one.

With an effort, Rook shifted his gaze from Beau's back to look for the boyish speaker. Blurrily in the blue-green twilight beneath the trees he could see that yes, it was the Sheriff's son, freckles and all. Tod. There he sat, at ease with his back against a hemlock trunk, his hurt leg wrapped in a splint, and a whole cooked partridge in his hands to gnaw upon.

Runkling grunted and tugged at his tether, trying to get at the partridge. A pig will eat almost anything.

Beau told Tod indignantly, "Stink? *Non, non,* the *petit* piggy, it smell better than you do."

"Well, something stinks."

"That would be Rook." She flashed her lightning grin over her shoulder at him.

He did not smile back. What did they expect? A creature of the wild did not stand in the rain and scrub itself, or bathe itself in the river. Rook was a wild thing, and he smelled how he smelled.

"Rook," said a soft voice.

Rowan, here, with Robin's band? Rook raised his head to look for her. Yes, there she stood, a straight arrow of a girl in her green kirtle. Foggily Rook remembered things Beau had been telling him, Sheriff's son this and Sheriff's son that, Rowan tending the boy's broken leg and Robin Hood's whole band with her, on the lookout and on the move in case the Sheriff himself came charging into the forest with a hundred knights swinging battle-axes, trying to get his wretched Tod back.

Although so far nothing of the sort had happened. Which was odd.

"Rook, where did you go?" Rowan was saying with no trace of anger in her voice, only . . . some other emotion. Blinking, Rook tried to focus on her face, but it swam before his eyes like an oval moon in green twilight, and her mouth seemed to waver in her face as she spoke. "I thought maybe you'd been captured, maybe even killed. I was frightened. Why didn't you tell me—"

Hemlocks seemed to be lifting, drifting, swaying, and Rook's head felt afloat between their branches, and he blurted words he had never before spoken aloud. "A wolf roams where he will."

Rowan's grave eyes widened, filling his watery

world. She asked him softly, "Is that what you are, Rook? A wolf?"

Even her lack of anger reproached him. He wanted to say something, explain, but his mind felt like a dead fish bobbing in a black river. He stood there.

Rowan peered at him. "Are you all right?"

Sounding as if it spoke from very far away, a strange voice said, "Rowan, he saved my life. He fought a wild boar to save me."

Oh. It was Beau, serious for once.

Another faraway voice, Tod's, chattered, "He could have left me in the man trap. I didn't care then if he stank. Actually he didn't stink as bad that day."

"His head's wounded," Beau said. "He won't let me look at it."

Rook heard Rowan gasp, and he heard her say, "Contagion! No wonder it smells. It's festering. . . ."

He heard that much, but he couldn't see anything except darkness. He felt Runkling's tether slip from his hand, and he felt someone strong, maybe Lionel or Robin Hood, catch him as he fell.

Rook awoke to find himself lying on a soft bed of somebody's mantle spread over—over a thick layer of fallen hemlock needles, probably, for he looked up at hemlocks. And at someone bending over him—it was that wretch Tod, of all people. Sitting by Rook's side with his broken leg stretched out at an awkward angle, the Sheriff's son nodded at Rook and said, "Rowan had to go find some kind of herb or something for you, to doctor your stinky skull. I'm supposed to get the fever down. Like so." His hand reached into a leather bucket, then came up holding a sopping wet rag with which he mopped Rook's face.

Rook stiffened, wanting to tell the brat to stop, wanting to curse him, wanting to hit him, but it was all he could do just to turn his face away. Tod kept right on sloshing water at the side of Rook's head, his neck, his shoulder and chest. Rook sighed and found that he had no strength for anger; he lay limp. The water's cool touch felt good, cleared his head. Able to think a little, he whispered, "Where's Runkling?"

"Runkling?"

"My . . . pig . . ."

"What, that suckling pork you brought us?" spoke another, deeper voice with a wink of laughter in it. Robin Hood crouched beside Tod, took the wet rag and started applying it to parts of Rook that Tod couldn't reach. " 'Twas the tenderest, most succulent roast I've ever tasted, lad, but barely enough for a bite apiece. Next time—"

"Bah. Don't listen to the lying scoundrel." But Tod's tone was as cheerful as Robin's. "Runkling, come here, pig." Tod swiveled to reach behind him, heaving something up in both hands. It squealed and kicked at the air with small pointed trotters. Tod held Runkling up so that Rook could see him, then set him back down on the ground. "Robin's been feeding him milk and bread," he said.

"To fatten him," Robin Hood explained with gravest drollery. "Even Tykell doesn't want to eat such a little bit of a runt. He looked at that so-called pig and—"

"Tykell *did* want to eat it," Tod put in. "But Rowan told him to let it be. And he listened to her. Even this proud oaf"—he flapped a hand toward Robin Hood—"listens to Rowan. Did you know that he's Rowan's *father*? I can't believe it. She's so nice, and he's such a smirking, stinging gadfly of a—"

"Bah," Rook growled. He knew Tod was not speaking to him, really, just carrying on some sort of game with Robin Hood. Less than a fortnight the Sheriff's son had been in the hands of Robin and his merry men, and already the brat was everyone's pet. A barbed feeling in Rook's chest gave him strength to tell Tod, "Go home if you don't like it here."

"I will," Tod said. "My father will come looking for me. My father will find me."

"Taking his time, isn't he?" Robin Hood teased.

The boy looked Robin straight in the eye. "Likely he's got important matters to attend to. With the king, belike."

"Belike." Robin's voice turned gentle, like the touch with which he swabbed Rook's legs. "But no need to wait for him, lad. As soon as we get you on crutches, we can guide you back to Nottingham."

Tod lowered his eyes, silent.

"Sooth, I could carry you there now on my back," said Robin, watching Tod.

Silence. Still staring at the ground, Tod took water from the bucket with one hand and smoothed it onto Rook's forehead. Rook let him do this.

"Tod, lad," said Robin, "tell me the truth." In his voice were the power and pity that made him Robin Hood. "The day we found you on that great black brute of a warhorse, what were you doing in the forest? Were you running away from your father?"

Tod took a long breath, swallowed, then straightened and faced Robin. "I suppose so. But I wanted to go back with—with a head hanging from the saddle."

He winced as if Robin Hood might hit him, but Robin only nodded. "You wanted to kill an outlaw?"

"Yes. To please him. To make him proud of me."

Don't laugh at me, Tod's face begged.

But Robin showed no sign of merriment, only puzzlement. "But you're a fine, sharp dagger of a lad, bright and bold. How is he not proud of you already?"

"I . . ." Quite suddenly Tod reached for Runkling and held the little pig on his lap, hugging it. "I don't know," he said to the top of Runkling's bristly head.

Rook hated the feeling in his chest, as if the thorny muddle there were making him bleed inside. A creature of the wild does not feel such pain. A wolf does not care what happens to others. Yet Rook could not help blurting a question at the Sheriff's son. "What will happen when you go back?"

Tod met his eyes without hesitation. "He will beat me for taking the horse. That's all." Tod reached for the cloth, and Robin gave it to him. Tod dunked it in the bucket, lifted it out and held it so that cool water dripped into Rook's clotted, knotted mane of hair. Rook closed his eyes.

Eight

❧

"N o," Rook said.

"But Rook, I have to cut some of your hair anyway to drain the wound and bandage it." In the orange campfire light, under the towering darkness of the hemlock trees, Rowan looked as steely as Rook had ever seen her. "Toads take it, Rook, any dolt knows too much hair saps your strength if you're sick. I am going to cut it all off."

Rook had not told her, yet somehow she knew: He felt as weak as a butterfly. But just the same, he mumbled, *"No."* Rook had not combed or washed or cut even the forelock of his hair since the day his father— since that day. The day that had made him an outlaw, a wolf's head, a wild boy of the woods. Confound it, Ettarde had always been wanting to cut his black clotted hair, or comb it or wash it, and he hadn't given in to her. And now Rowan—he had never thought Rowan would turn against him so. Defiance gave Rook enough strength to sit up, although his head spun with the effort and the stench of his own contagion filled his nostrils and made him nauseous. "A wolf doesn't . . ." He blurred the words, and stopped himself from saying more, but Rowan heard.

"A wolf?" She leaned closer to him, kneeling, her face level with his. "Rook, you are not a wolf. You are a person, a swineherd's son." His face must have changed when she said this, for her voice softened. "Tod told us."

Rook turned his head, and yes, there was the Sheriff's freckled brat sitting nearby with his broken leg stretched out, holding Runkling on his lap. Scratching the little pig along the backbone and behind the ears. Runkling lay snoring with pleasure, his eyes closed. Rook noticed what long eyelashes the shoat had. And he noticed Tod's silence, and the look in Tod's eyes. Tod met Rook's glaring stare with—was that pleading? The young snot had not begged when he was dying in the man trap, yet he was begging for something now?

Rowan added, "My father was friends with your father, Rook, did you know that?"

"I knew him well," said Robin Hood's voice out of the hemlock shadows. "Everyone knew Jack Pigkeep. A man of few words, wisely spoken. A man with a strong back, a brave arm and a generous heart. I should have guessed before now that you are his son."

Painful memories twisted in Rook's gut, made him bare his teeth in a snarl.

Rowan repeated, "You are his son, Rook. Would your father want you to act like a wild beast?"

"Don't speak of him!"

Silence. Silence so deep, Rook could sense the breathing of dozens of outlaws all around him, in the shadows amid the sheltering trees.

"All right," said Rowan softly. "But would a wolf wear a strand of my ring, Rook?"

It was as if the contagion had put poison into Rook's heart; he wanted to snatch the silver strand resting on his bare chest, tear it off and fling it away. But he had strength only to turn his face away from Rowan, trying to lie down. He wanted to be let alone. He wanted to rest. The poisonous feeling passed through him and left him feeling watery, with no retorts in him.

Rowan's gentle hands were yet strong enough to hold him where he was, sitting upright. "You are not a wild beast," Rowan said. "You are one of us."

Undeniably so. Yet Rook shook his head as if he felt flies bothering him.

An outlaw called from the shadows, "Rowan, he's not in his right mind. Do you want us to hold him down while you cut—"

"No!" A fresh jolt of rage gave Rook strength to shout even though Rowan waved the outlaw's offer away. "No, I'll die first!"

Rowan appealed, "Rook, for the love of mercy . . ."

"*Sacre amour* of the toad, Rook," came Beau's mocking voice, "for what is to be so stubborn? Here." She strode out of the shadows to kneel facing him, beside Rowan. "Look." She pulled her dagger, seized a long hank of her own hair with her other hand, and sliced. Her bleached-blond tresses fell away, leaving black stubble. "See?" She sliced again, laying more long, bleached hair on the ground at her feet. "Is not so hard! Rowan, you do the back?"

"You want it all off?" Rowan's face looked as if she were studying some new creature she had not seen before.

"*Mais oui,* of course."

Between the two of them they finished the job quickly. On the ground lay a mess of long blond curls, all that was left of Beau's former life as the high king's page boy. On Beau's head stood stubble as raven-black as Rook's long tangled mane of hair. She flashed Rook her most shining glance, gave him her most dazzling grin. "Now you do it. And then we be twins, yes?"

Rook saw one of Rowan's rare smiles quirking at the corners of her mouth as she studied Beau. "Twin brothers?"

"Your turn, *mon frère*." Beau offered Rook her dagger.

He stared at it. Filigree hand guard. Carved hilt. A crystal globe of chalcedony in the pommel. The dagger with which she had killed a wild boar and saved his life.

And now she was trying to save him again. Let him cut his black tangled mane of hair himself. Save his pride.

She continued to offer the dagger with patience as unusual, coming from her, as her silence. No one spoke. The only sound Rook heard was Runkling snoring, still being patted by that proud brat—

Brat? Who was being proud now?

Rook blinked, then shakily reached for the dagger. He fumbled his fingers onto the filigree handle and lifted the blade to his hair, but his hands wavered so much, he knew he was as likely to cut off an ear as not. He lowered his hand and passed the dagger to Rowan. "You do it," he mumbled.

He noticed that she said nothing either to scold him or praise him. Silently he thanked her for her silence as she started to shear away the long tangles. Her touch could not have been more gentle.

Bracing himself with both hands to stay upright, Rook found it difficult to remind himself that a creature of the wild does not need friends.

Nine

❧

Rook awoke to find himself lying at ease in a bed of piled furs, looking up at sunlit treetops—but not hemlock. Feathery fronds of rowan whispered overhead, and from somewhere close by, a murmur of living water answered them. Even before he sat up, Rook knew where he was: the rowan hollow.

Sitting up was more of a task than it should have been. Rook had to hoist himself with both hands. He felt as feeble as a mouse. Vaguely he remembered the sickening stench as Rowan had opened the wound to clean the poison out, the sickening pain that had made him fall over in a faint—but there was no pain now. He remembered lying half dead with fever—but there was no fever in him now. Breeze on his shorn head felt fresh and cool. He was wearing somebody's jerkin, and a blanket covered his legs, and he actually felt as if he needed the warmth of them.

"Hungry?" asked the voice he expected. He turned to find Rowan's warm, grave gaze on him.

Rook shook his head. He felt more muddled than hungry. "How am I here?"

"Lionel carried you. I thought you would do better here." Sitting in the shelter of the rocks with her wolf-dog by her side, Rowan tilted her head toward the ever-running spring that welled at the heart of the rowan hollow. And yes, Rook knew with a bone-deep instinct, it was Rowan's spring that had soothed the fever out of him. That and Rowan herself, her touch. Which was almost the same thing. Rowan was at one with this place, the rowan grove.

"Tod's all right without me now, I hope," Rowan added, stroking Tykell.

To his wonder, Rook found that he hoped so too.

"*Sacre bleu* toads," called a glad voice from the rocks, "*mon cher frère,* my twin brother, he awakes!"

Rook sighed and rolled his eyes as Beau thumped down to land on booted feet beside him, with Runkling in her arms.

"Put him down," Rook grumbled. "Let him root."

"*Mais non,* he root up the whole forest and plough it

into a field for the, what you call it, the turnips!" Beau flashed her most wicked grin. "I take him to Fountain Dale, let him root there. Next year we grow parsnips."

From behind Rook, a familiar peevish voice said, "Belle has found her calling."

"No call me Belle!" Beau flared. "No ding-dong!"

Rook looked around to find Lionel towering over him, a whole dead fallow deer on his shoulders. Lionel would kill meat and bring it home, but somebody else had to butcher it; Lionel had a tremendous stomach for eating, but no stomach at all for gutting and skinning.

"Belle has become a paragon among piggy-sitters," Lionel told Rook.

Beau yelled, "So Tykell no eat Runkling!"

Fear jolted Rook. He shot a look at the wolf-dog, and yes, Tykell was eyeing the young pig hungrily. Rowan's hand lay on his back to restrain him.

"You stop it to call me Belle," Beau ordered Lionel.

"When you stop it to speak that phony accent," Lionel mimicked, easing the dead deer from his shoulders to the ground. "My dear little Belle."

Belle set Runkling down and drew her dagger, wagged it like a scolding finger at Lionel, then bent to skin the deer. Snorting happily, Runkling trotted to Rook, and he hugged the piglet, all bristles and sharp trotters, in his arms. Something swelled inside his chest, making him feel even wobblier than before. He lay down, Runkling in his arms, blinking up at rowan fronds with hints of bud showing already; in a few weeks the trees would flower heavenly white.

Rook had never bedded in the rowan grove before. He had kept to himself in his caves in the rocks nearby. In a few days, when he felt better, he assured himself, he would move back to one of his caves, and his hair would grow again, and things would be as they were before.

Except . . . it felt like an embrace to have the rowan hollow around him, with its ever-flowing spring and the warm blaze of the campfire and Lionel bringing more wood in, still bickering with Beau, as Rowan materialized like a good spirit beside Rook to study him.

"Hungry?" she asked again.

Rook nodded.

A few days later, even though he felt much stronger, Rook stayed in the rowan hollow with the others. Any time now, he told himself, he would go back to his cave. Be on his own again, except that he'd take Runkling with him. In a day or two.

He napped a lot, with Runkling snoring by his side.

One sunny afternoon he napped so well that he awoke to find that night had already fallen. The campfire burned low and warm, sending aromas of ember-baked bread and roasting partridge into the night. In the fire's tawny glow sat Robin Hood, visiting with Rowan.

"What think you?" he was asking as she studied some kind of staff he was showing to her.

She stood up and tucked its fur-padded Y-shaped end under her arm. "Handsomely done, once you've trimmed it."

"How? Trimmed it where?"

"Trimmed it for Tod's height."

" 'Tis the right height."

"Then it couldn't be better." She swung the crutch by gripping a stub halfway down its shaft. "What most people forget is the handle." A branch cut to the right length, its end whittled round. Robin Hood had made this crutch for Tod by searching out a young tree with the right natural form, then cutting and shaping it, the way Rook had made a boar spear. But Robin had taken great pains with polishing and smoothing, so much so that Rook pushed Runkling aside and sat up to take a better look.

"Rook, lad!" Robin turned to him at once. "How are you?"

A creature of the wild does not care how it feels. But the breeze blew sweet through the rowans. And on the breeze floated music even sweeter, the honey-golden notes of Lionel's harp. Rook could not help but feel blessed. He gave Robin a quiet look and a nod.

Runkling awoke with a grunt, scrabbled up and trotted to Robin Hood, his tail twirling. Selecting a stick from the kindling pile, Robin rubbed the tip of it along Runkling's back. Stiff-legged, with his eyes closed, Runkling stood groaning in porcine ecstasy.

Robin Hood, scratching a pig? Rook blurted, "You know swine?"

Robin smiled, his eyes sparkling in the firelight. "I know many swine. The king's foresters, bounty hunters, Guy of Gisborn, Lord Roderick, the Sheriff of Nottingham . . ." But then his grin faded. Still looking at the piglet, he said quietly, "Yes, I used to help your father with his swine from time to time. Rook, lad, I am ashamed of myself."

The harp music hit a startled sour note, then ceased. "What?" exclaimed voices from the darkness beyond the campfire—Beau, Lionel. Rowan stood stone still, the crutch still under her arm, staring at her father. Rook's mouth opened, but no sound came out. Somewhere in the tree-thick darkness an owl hooted as if it were laughing at the very idea: Robin Hood, ashamed? Unheard of. He had to be joking, or playing one of his tricks.

But he didn't seem to be. He laid his pig-scratching stick aside and turned to face Rook. "I saw you in the forest many times with your father," he said. "We didn't want to burden you with knowledge of outlaws and such, lad, but your father and I would talk when you weren't looking. He was proud of how you helped him and never complained, how you shortened the days for him, always chattering and laughing and singing. . . ."

"What!" Beau and Lionel exclaimed anew. Rowan laid the crutch on the ground and walked over to sit beside Rook as if she thought he might need her. As if she knew how his stomach had turned to quivering water, remembering those days that seemed to have taken place in a different person's life.

Far off in the wilderness night a rabbit screamed, dying in the fangs of a fox, or maybe a wolf. Rook tightened his jaw.

"You had your hair cut short so it wouldn't catch in the bushes," Robin was saying. "You were a fine, strong lad helping your father, running with the shoats, herding them by playing with them. I remember you climbing trees in a warm sheepskin cape and sheepskin leggings, a yellow cap on your head, happy as the day was long."

Rook gave only a growl, a warning.

Robin nodded a kind of acknowledgment. "My men and I were roaming Barnesdale forest, north of here, when it happened," he said. "We heard about Jack Woodsby when we wandered back this way." Robin's eyes winced. "But I never heard what had happened to Jack's son, the boy he called Runkling. I thought most likely someone from the village had taken him in."

"Oh," Rowan whispered; Rook heard her close to his side. "Oh, I see."

Rook began to see, also, why Robin Hood had said he was ashamed, but understanding did not help him. Dark, barbed emotions raked his heart.

Robin Hood looked him in the eyes and said it. "All this time, I didn't know you."

"But Father, no one could have known." Rowan leaned toward him. "From what you say, he'd changed so. . . ."

Robin's blue-eyed gaze shifted to Rowan, and Rook had never seen those eyes so shadowed, like deep water.

"That's what harrows me the most, how his father's death changed him. I can scarcely imagine—the pain."

Pain? A wild thing feels no pain. Deep in Rook's chest his growl rumbled louder.

"Rook." Robin faced him again. "There's only one comfort I can offer you, not nearly enough, but here it is. When we heard what had happened to Jack By-the-Woods, my men and I went and found the man trap. We took your father from it. We carried him to a certain grove and buried him there and marked the place with a stone and said the blessing of the Lady over him."

Rook felt his growling stop for a moment—along with his breath. He felt his soul turning and turning like an eddying pool, felt himself floating like a maple wing, could have gone lilting in sky like a butterfly or swimming in greenshadow like a trout or flowing wherever the river took him, no bitter blackthorn tangle in his chest, nothing but . . .

Nothing. Fearsome nothingness, as if he were a dead, dried cattle-bean pod and would blow away in the wind.

Robin Hood said, "Anytime you want me to, I will take you and show you the place where your father lies."

Somewhere in the wild distance, a wolf howled as if

its heart would break. Rook breathed out, stood up and stumbled back from Robin, the campfire, the others. Runkling trotted to him, giving a snouty smile, but Rook wanted no smiles. He clenched his fists, his teeth. A welter of feelings, sharp, dark, barbed, surged back to fill the terrifying emptiness within his chest. Good. Thorns were good, brambles were good. A wild thing needs a thicket in which to lie and lick its wounds.

Scooping up Runkling with one hand, Rook climbed out of the rowan hollow and strode into the night, heading toward his cold cave. He did not look back.

No one would follow. They knew better.

Ten

Three days later, Rook huddled in his favorite cave, sharing his breakfast with Runkling and telling himself things were back the way he wanted them. No more bandages and blankets and jerkins on him. Bare-shouldered. No more nursemaids. Alone. Breakfast was cold undercooked grayling left over from the day before, when he'd caught it with his bare, cold hands and fixed it himself.

And then he hadn't felt very hungry for it. Nor did he this morning. Runkling seemed to savor the fish a good deal more than Rook did.

Rook heard a soft footstep outside the cave, and knew who it was even before she peered in: Rowan, with her brown braid hanging down as she bent to check on him. "Toads!" she grumbled. "Why are you feeding that pig?"

Rook shrugged. He knew Runkling found plenty to eat in the forest, especially squirmy things he grubbed up from underground. But he offered Runkling the last of the fish anyway, and the shoat slobbered all over his hand as he gulped it.

"I'm not hungry," Rook said.

"I know, but you have to eat, Rook! You're as thin and pale as morning mist. Go down to the hollow; we have bread and cheese. Or should I tell Beau to bring you some?"

He shook his head. These days there was a clotted feeling in his belly all the time, and nothing tasted good.

Rowan crouched at the entrance of his cave, giving him her steadiest grave-eyed gaze.

"I'm all right," he told her.

She shook her head. "You can't go on being a wolf, Rook. Too much has happened."

Her calm gaze as much as her words frightened him. There was something in her eyes of a peace he couldn't bear.

"You're going to have to come out of your lair," she said.

How could she live with such quiet in her heart? Rook growled, and his lips pulled back from his clenched teeth.

Then he felt Runkling press against his side, stiff and quivering, as a louder growl sounded in answer. At the mouth of the cave crouched Tykell, his yellow eyes on the piglet. The wolf-dog took a creeping, stalking pace toward Runkling.

"Ty!" Rowan snapped more sharply than Rook had ever heard her speak to anyone who was not her enemy. She nearly shouted. "Tykell, I told you, let Runkling alone!"

Tykell shrank back, suddenly looking like a puppy caught piddling on the floor. He gave Rowan a hurt look, and then with a flip of his plumy tail he loped away, disappearing into the forest.

Rowan gazed after him, puffing her lips in exasperation. "Toads take it," she muttered, "now he's got his parlous large nose out of joint, I won't see him for three days. *Stinking* toads."

Runkling ran to her with soft grunts, and she patted him absently, shifting her attention back to Rook. "And you're just as bad," she complained. "You won't eat, you're going to get sick again, and between you and Tod I'm out of feverfew, yarrow, knitbone, agrimony, everything." With a decided gesture she stood up. "I'd better go to the meadows and see what I can find." Walking away, she called back, "Rook, for the love of the Lady, eat something? Please?"

He didn't. He lay in his cave, while Runkling snored beside him, and watched the angle of the sunlight move. He didn't care whether he caught more fish to eat. He couldn't think of anything he cared about, anything he wanted to do. The sun had passed overhead and slanted toward afternoon before an odd rhythmic sound roused him.

It was a kind of hitch-thump followed by a scraping sort of footfall, coming up the rocky slope toward his cave.

Rook sat up, his hands brushing his face from habit, although there was no shaggy mane of hair in his eyes now. He scowled as if something had hurt him, then crawled to the cave's entrance to look.

It was Tod, on his crutch, heading up the tor all alone.

Laboring over the crags, Tod kept his eyes on the uneven ground. But when Rook slipped out of his cave and stood, Tod looked up at him.

"Hullo," he said. "They told me I'd find you up here."

Runkling trotted out of the cave and ran to Tod, his short tail wagging with excitement as he snorted a greeting. Rook just stared.

"Beau and Lionel told me," Tod chattered on. "Rowan's not there. She went to find herbs. I wanted to see her too." He stood before Rook, leaning on his crutch and panting, but his voice quieted as he mentioned Rowan, and a shadow darkened his bright eyes. "Will you tell her I said thank you? And good-bye?"

Rook felt his jaw drop.

Tod said, "I'm going back to Nottingham tomorrow."

Rook felt his insides sloshing like a butter churn. Out of the splatter he forced a single word. "Why?"

Tod stared at him.

"To be beaten?" Rook grumped.

Tod looked at the ground, sighed and slumped down to sit. Runkling rubbed against him, and he gathered the piglet into his arms.

"I don't know what else to do," he told Rook.

Rook crouched to glare at him.

"My father will come to find me," Tod said. "I mean, really. He will. Sometime. And . . . and I don't want him to hurt . . ." Tod hesitated, swallowed hard, then said it. "I don't want him to hurt Robin. Or anyone."

Glaring was easy. Trying to think what to say was hard. Rook continued to glare.

"Robin made me this crutch," Tod said.

Rook nodded.

"He and Little John will carry me to the Nottingham Way," Tod said. "It's not far from there. I can walk the rest of the way." He hugged Runkling, ruffled the pig's ears, then set him aside and struggled to his feet. He looked straight into Rook's glowering eyes. "Rook, I came to thank you for not leaving me in that man trap. I know you really wanted to. Thank you for letting me live."

A muddy brown flood of feelings made Rook look away. He heard Tod say, "Good-bye," but he couldn't reply. He couldn't lift his glare from the ground. He heard Tod starting to crutch away—

A whistle as shrill as a hawk's scream soared over Sherwood Forest.

Rook leapt to his feet, snatching at his dagger. Tod stood like a startled deer. Maybe he remembered hearing that signal before—for his own sake.

"Is it—is somebody caught in a man trap?" he gasped, his face fish-belly pale under the freckles.

Rook didn't answer, because he didn't know the answer. His mind squirreled, and he couldn't think what he should do. He knew only that something was badly wrong, and he ran headlong down the crags toward the alarm signal. One of Robin Hood's men, maybe, had been hurt or captured. Or, far worse, could it be Beau, or Lionel, or—

No. He was a wild thing. He wouldn't think it, or care, or feel his heart bursting with dread of—

"Rook, wait!" cried Tod.

That cry might not have halted him, but his own dread did. He turned to bark something at Tod, and saw the boy trying to run after him, his crutch flailing. Then its tip caught, and Tod pitched forward, fell, and kept on falling, crashing against stones as he tumbled down the tor, clutching at brush and rocks that ripped out of his hands. Rook saw blood even before Tod thumped to a stop against a boulder.

The boy didn't make a sound, and at first Rook thought he was dead. He ran toward him.

But as Rook reached Tod, the boy sat up, bruised and scraped, with his lips pressed together. Rook had forgotten: The Sheriff's son was brave.

Heart thudding, Rook bent to help him up—but another hand reached down. Rook had not seen even a shadow, had not heard so much as the scrape of a footfall on stone or a pebble rattling, but there stood Robin Hood.

"Tod, lad. Come, hurry. On my back." Robin hoisted Tod and strode off.

Rook grabbed up Tod's crutch from the ground and trotted after them. "What has happened?" he growled at Robin.

Robin did not answer. And glancing at Robin's face, seeing his hard jaw and his shadowed eyes, Rook did not dare to speak again.

Tod did, his voice small and scared. "Robin?"

"Tod, lad." Robin spoke to him gently, as always, but his voice was as taut as a stretched leather shield. "There's been a change in plans. I'm going to have to exchange you as a hostage, lad."

Rook stared.

Tod blurted, "Why? Who . . ."

"Your father has captured Rowan."

Eleven

At the edge of the forest near Nottingham, Robin Hood's outlaw band had gathered, their lips tight, their hands tight on their bows, not speaking as their leader joined them.

"Anything?" Robin asked. The high road to Nottingham curved near Sherwood at that point. As far as Rook could understand from what little Robin Hood had said, Rowan had been taken by a patrol on sortie to the north as she searched for herbs on the meadows at the forest's edge. The patrol would pass here as they returned, triumphant, with their captive.

"Soon. I hope." Little John's voice sounded so level and quiet that Rook started to shake. "But nothing yet. Only what yon foreigner said." He pointed with his bearded chin.

At first Rook thought he saw a slim, pale boy stand-ing in the shadow—but no. It was Beau. He hadn't recognized her without her smile.

"What I said was the truth." Trembling, her voice betrayed the slight accent of a Wanderer, an outcast without a country. "The Sheriff's men surrounded us. They knew who she was; they called her Rowan Hood. They taunted her that they would take her alive to make best use of her."

A year ago Rowan would have passed as just another cowherd's daughter or goose girl, but now . . . too much had happened. The man trap. Her legs, hurt so she couldn't run and dodge as she used to. The bounty hunters, finding out who she was. And now, by the looks of things, somehow Nottingham had heard as well.

Rowan, captured . . . Rook shook his head, trying to shake his hurtful thoughts away. He felt he was to blame. Because she'd been gathering herbs on account of him. Because, on account of him and Runkling, Tykell had not been there to guard her or protect her.

Beau kept talking as if she could not help it, as if she had to keep telling and telling what had happened. "I— I couldn't move, but Rowan got her bow strung. She sent elf-bolts into . . ." Beau swallowed hard at the memory. "Into three of them. They fell, and she shouted at me to run. She . . . she commanded me."

Robin Hood nodded, but his blue eyes looked faraway gray. He set Tod on his feet. On his one good foot, rather.

Beau whispered, "There was nothing else I could do."

"I know, lass," Robin said quietly. No one else answered her. Rook tried to give her a look and a nod, but he couldn't. Terror for Rowan crouched like a hooded hawk in his belly, its knife-sharp claws gripping his innards.

Clutching at a tree for support, Tod gazed up at Robin, then turned to Rook with eyes like those of a hunted deer. After a moment Rook felt the crutch still in his grasp and handed it to the boy.

"Where's Lionel?" asked Robin hoarsely. "Just when we need his strength the most . . ."

"Hsst," breathed Little John. "Hearken. Look."

Every outlaw froze, peering. Rook could see it too, a puff of dust in the distance, growing nearer. Then he heard the trampling of horses, and the harsh voices of the men-at-arms. And amid the dust he saw glints of bronze. Brazen helms. And the Sheriff's ornate breastplate. On a heavy-headed charger, Nottingham rode in the fore.

Then Rook saw Rowan, and his stomach clenched like a fist. They rode horseback, but they made her go afoot, tethered by a rope long enough to put her behind their horses' tails, in the thick of their dust. Trotting to keep up, she panted, coughing, sweat streaking the dirt on her face. Blood stained her mouth. They had struck her. Rook felt as if he had himself been struck. But what hurt his heart was the way she held her head high even as she struggled along. Chin up, defiant, she looked like a true outlaw. Like her father.

"Lady have mercy," he breathed. Would they hang her? Tod might expect to be beaten when he returned home, but what would they do to Rowan?

"Lad?" Robin looked down at Tod.

Staring at Rowan, the boy swallowed hard, then nodded and crutched forward. Weaponless, Robin walked with him. Rook stood with the others, his dagger lifted in his trembling hand; it was his only weapon. He'd been too much a lone wolf to learn to shoot the bow like the others.

Tod stood in the middle of the road with Robin Hood by his side. They waited.

Nottingham rounded the curve—and saw them.

Hand on Tod's shoulder, Robin called, "Sir Sheriff!"

It was the signal. The outlaws stepped forward, just

out of their leafy cover, presenting a score of arrows nocked to fly. Nottingham yanked his charger to a halt, his armor jangling, and his patrol stopped behind him.

"An exchange of prisoners, Sir Sheriff, if you please," said Robin Hood.

Staring at Tod, the Sheriff barely blinked.

"Your son," said Robin.

"For your daughter?" At first the Sheriff's meaty face creased; then he roared with raging laughter. "You think I want my wretched runt of a son? That horse thief? Do you think I care what you do to him?"

Rook heard a strange, choked sound he could not at first understand. Had it come from Tod? Yes. The Sheriff's son, he who had not whimpered in the man trap—now he cried out in pain.

And his father seemed not to notice at all, his narrow glittering stare on Robin Hood. "No, there's only one head I want for your daughter's," he said, one hard word at a time between grinning teeth. "Or along with it. Yours!" He lifted a gauntleted hand in sudden angry command. "Kill him! Slay the wolf's head!"

Robin lunged for the forest, taking Tod with him, crutch and all, shielding the boy with his body as the men-at-arms drew their bows. But a volley of gray goose-fletched arrows from the outlaws flew first.

"Don't hit Rowan!" Rook tried to shout. His voice came out more like a frog's croak. But as he spoke, Rowan ran forward to shield herself amid the horses. Or—no, she was weaving between them, winding her tether around their hocks, setting them to bucking. A man-at-arms grabbed her from behind. She twisted out of his grasp and stepped right under his horse to pop up on the other side. With a rope slithering against its belly, the horse reared, dumping the rider. Even with her arms bound tight to her sides, Rowan was keeping her head.

Rook's terror for her gave him strength to run forward, dagger drawn, with no thought except to cut that rope away from her.

But already he knew he would never reach her. He was too small amid dust and yells and the pounding of his own heart and hooves pounding toward him and someone's great heavy sword swishing down on him. He would die—

With a roar like that of a maddened bull, something massive charged between him and the sword, knocking it skyward and him onto the ground as it hurtled toward Rowan.

"Lionel! It's Lionel! Save her," someone yelled like a lunatic—Rook barely recognized the voice as his own.

Struggling up, he saw an arrow *thwok* into the back of Lionel's shoulder. It appeared to only annoy Lionel. His roar rose to a scream of rage. The mounted guardsman grasping Rowan's tether confronted him with leveled spear, but Lionel brushed the weapon aside and ran the man down, attacking barehanded like a lion, a bear, a boar, knocking the horse off its feet as he wrenched the rope free. He didn't give the flattened horse and rider another glance. Wasting no time, he picked up Rowan, rope and all, hugged her to his great chest and barreled off with her, leaping like an elk into Sherwood Forest.

Running in that wilderness, Lionel could outdistance any rider on horseback. Rowan was safe.

"Rook, come on!" Someone grabbed his elbow; it was Beau. "Run!" She yanked him toward the forest.

"Scatter!" Robin Hood shouted, and as if a covey of partridge had burst into flight, Sherwood Forest roiled with confusion. For a long time Rook ran alone and at random, panting, heartbeat pounding in his ears. Sore afraid, even though he knew the Sheriff's men would not separate for fear of ambush, and could not pursue them all, and could not move amid the trees on horseback as quickly as a man on foot. As Rook ran, he could hear the Sheriff of Nottingham cursing—close behind him at first, then farther away. Rook dodged deep, deeper into the forest, running until he could run no farther, then pausing to pant as he looked around for someplace to hide.

There. A thickly spreading oak with just enough knobbiness on its mighty trunk.

Rook climbed, but it wasn't as easy as it should have been. His brief burst of strength had passed. He hadn't eaten in too long. He felt weak. Instead of scooting like a squirrel up the oak, the best he could do was crawl up, gripping like a badger. He hadn't yet reached the concealment of the foliage when he heard men's voices behind him.

"I hear one of them!"

"Where?"

"Yonder!" They crashed toward Rook.

Rook heaved himself to the first big branch, still in plain view, still an easy shot for someone's arrow. Terror shook him worse than ever. Even a wild creature does not want to die. Hoofbeats sounded, brush crashed, and Rook could not help looking over his shoulder as four of Nottingham's men burst into sight.

But not one of them glanced up to see him. They all

gawked straight past the trunk of his tree, and one of them gave a hoarse yell: "Wolves!" They hauled on their reins, stopping their horses.

What wolves? Where? Rook had not seen any. But the men-at-arms snatched for their bows to shoot a hasty spate of arrows. Rook heard the swish of brush, a yelp of pain. The men relaxed.

"That sent them running."

"It was wolves you heard, dolt."

"Somebody got one."

"Leave it. It's outlaws we're after. Come on!"

Without pausing to reclaim their spent arrows, they cantered off.

Rook clung to his tree, panting with weariness and relief, as they rode away. He heard something whimper, and at first he thought it was him. Then he saw the wolf trying to drag itself to cover. It crawled only a short way before it collapsed on the roots of his tree, head flat on the ground, its ribs heaving, a yellow-feathered arrow jutting waspish between them.

Rook had never seen a wolf so plainly before, although he had seen the pigs they killed, sometimes right in the pigsty. Since he had become an outlaw, a few times he had seen gray shadows flitting. Mostly he had heard fearsome howls in the night. But this wolf didn't look fearsome. With its ears flattened in pain, it seemed like a long-legged gray dog lying there.

He heard a whine, and a smaller, darker wolf trotted to the dying one and bent to lick its face. A mate? Or a half-grown pup, a daughter, a son?

Brush rattled, branches snapped, and three big red deer bounded past—frightened from their thickets by Nottingham's men, most likely. The dark wolf did not even give the deer a glance. It stood for a moment with its proud head bowed. Then it curled up close against the other one, licking its eyes and ears.

Rook bit his lip. He remembered wiping sweat from his father's face as his father lay in the man trap. He remembered some of the sounds his father had made, dying. And some of the sounds he, Runkling, Jack's son, had made.

The wounded wolf shuddered and stopped breathing. The arrow's yellow tuft of feathers grew still.

Rook didn't want to watch anymore. He turned his face upward and climbed. The first wolf had gone silent, but the dark wolf whimpered as if it were weeping.

Twelve

Rook crawled up the tree and settled himself in a muscular, comfortable crook of bough. Far above the ground, blanketed with foliage, he lay at ease as the tree held him like a mother cradling a baby.

Or like a father.

Far below, the dark wolf howled, grieving. Could the dead one be its father?

Stop it. Think no more of fathers.

Looking for something else to rest his mind upon, Rook glanced around him—but then he saw the rowan. Close to where he curled in the tree's embrace, far above the ground, a rowan seed had taken root on the oak, and now a rowan sapling grew right out of the massive tree's broad shoulders. White blossoms were beginning to froth on the rowan's feathery boughs, so that it stood like a dove, feet on the oak and head high in the sky. Every rowan was goodly, but this one seemed almost magical. A flying rowan, the country folk would have called it.

Rowan Hood, Rook thought, *and Robin's the oak.*

Robin Hood. Her father.

Fair, kind, mighty. A father worthy of any child's dream.

I had such a father. Jack-o-Shoats, Jack Pigkeep, Jack Woodsby, gentle and brave. Until the Sheriff of Nottingham doomed him to die.

But Tod . . . Tod's father *was* the Sheriff.

Which of us is worse off?

Was it perhaps better to have a kindly father, dead, than a cruel one, alive?

All that day Rook hid in the oak. Twice more he heard the rattle and swish of frightened deer running through the forest. And twice more horseback riders passed beneath him. Nottingham's men. The first time, he heard their shouts as the dark wolf ran away from them. The second time he heard only their hoofbeats, the creaking of their saddles and the jingle of their armor. He did not bother to look down. He knew he could not see them and they could not see him. He was not afraid.

Except of the strange ideas in his mind. Some of his own thoughts made him cold with fear.

When twilight had deepened to dusk and promised nightfall, Rook slipped back down to the ground, avoiding the stiff body of the dead wolf. He stood just looking at it for a moment, wanting to back away, yet at the same time wanting to kneel and caress the gray fur.

Wolves, in stark daylight? What had they been doing here, just in time to keep Nottingham's men from spotting him?

Likely they had been frightened from their daytime hiding place, just like the deer. Yet Rook felt a warm shudder, a sense of presence, as if some spirit of Sherwood Forest had put an invisible arm around his shoulder.

"You saved my life," he whispered.

The wolf's dead eyes looked at him yet through him, past him, staring and empty. Soon the flies would come buzzing around them.

"Thank you," Rook murmured.

The wolf lay as flat as forever, with its mouth open,

its tongue hanging slack between its fangs. How many people had it killed with those fangs?

"Bah," Rook muttered, turning away. "Scare stories," he grumbled. False tales folk told, like the ones they told about outlaws. He could not imagine that the dead wolf had ever hurt anyone. No more than Tod—

"Bah!"

Fleeing his own thoughts, Rook strode into the forest.

He tried to walk quickly and found he could not. Too weak. His pace kept slowing. He needed to eat. But the clotted feeling in his belly had swollen until it hurt, and he walked on without foraging, because he knew he would not be able to eat until he had seen Rowan. Until he knew she was alive and well. She and the others.

He had to find them.

But he had no idea where they might be, whether at Robin Hood's oak dingle or the rowan hollow or the hemlock grove or some other place.

And it scarcely mattered, for he had no idea where in vast Sherwood Forest he was himself.

He walked on, wobbly on his feet. Perhaps if he kept moving, he would stumble across something, some landmark he knew. . . .

If he could see it. Which seemed unlikely. Night had fallen.

Dark. The whole world.

But then, far off in the darkness Rook heard a distant sound. Once, then again, then a third time, clear silver notes shining like a star to guide him.

He raised his head, took a deep breath, blinked water from his eyes and turned toward the music of Robin Hood's horn.

For a long, weary time he stumbled through the forest, banging his bare toes against hard things and scraping his bare shoulders against rough ones while thorns scratched his bare arms and legs until they bled. No matter; a creature of the wild didn't mind thorns.

But I do mind, whispered a traitor thought deep within Rook.

No. No, such thoughts were not allowed. A wild boy didn't care about thorns, or the pain of hunger, or the pain of wondering whether his friends were all right.

But I do care.

Rook remembered the dark wolf's whimper, the dark wolf's howl. He remembered the blood he had seen on Rowan's face, the arrow jutting from Lionel's shoulder, Beau's pale face as she tugged him away from danger. He remembered the way Tod had cried out—

He bit his lip as he struggled on.

Twice more Robin Hood's horn sounded its silver notes to guide him before at last he saw the campfire's warm golden light and recognized the place—the hollow with Robin Hood's giant oak spreading over it. Rook forgot to harden his face as he hurried the last few steps toward—Rowan, yes, Lady be thanked. It was Rowan turning toward him in the firelight, a strip of bandaging in her hands.

Everything blurred, and for a moment he couldn't see properly. But he heard many voices.

"There's Rook." One of Robin Hood's outlaws.

"Rook!" Rowan called. "Are you all right?"

"*Mon foi,* look, the poor Rook." Beau had her *accent faux* back. "All blood and blunder."

"He's done in," said another outlaw.

"Rook." Rowan touched his arm; even in the bleary darkness he knew the gentle power of her hand. "Sit down, let me look at you."

He sat, and felt a wet cloth wipe his face, felt her touch strengthening him, and blinked away wetness until he could see her kneeling beside him.

"I'm fine," she told him even though he had not spoken a word of his fears for her. "I wish I could start the day over and change it, that's all." He had never seen her face so bruised with sorrow as well as with blows. "Men dead because of me—"

"Do not say so, lass," came Little John's gruff voice somewhere behind him. "Only three badly wounded, and they might yet live. You have cared for them well."

Rowan pressed her trembling lips together and said nothing.

"John," complained a familiar voice, "she means Nottingham's men too." Leaning against the great oak, his shoulder bandaged and his arm in a sling, sat Lionel.

"Aye?" Rook could hear the shrug in Little John's voice. "Well, Lady be thanked, ours are all accounted for. And now Rook's back."

"Rook," said another voice, intense. Robin Hood crouched before him with—Lady have mercy, Robin was holding Runkling like a baby in his arms. "Rook, lad." Worry grayed Robin's eyes. "Have you seen aught of Tod?"

Rook just stared.

"Tod's not here," Robin Hood said. "No one saw where he went. Do you know where he is?"

Thirteen

It was nearly noon of the next day when Rook got up and walked away from Robin's camp with Runkling trotting at his bare heels.

"Are you running off again?" Rowan called after him. Harsh words, for her, but he accepted them without anger. She had been up all night tending to the wounded outlaws, Rook knew, and one of them had died. Robin and Little John were off in the forest somewhere, digging a grave. Some other outlaws were searching for Tod, but not many could be spared, not when their comrades were lying hurt. No one had much heart for the search. Tod could be anywhere, maybe even back in Nottingham. No one had seen Tykell either, so on top of everything else, Rowan missed her furry companion. . . . Turning to look at her, Rook saw sleepless nightmares of worry in her face.

So, even though a wolf roams where he will, Rook answered Rowan, if only with a shake of the head. No, he was not running off again.

Rowan frowned. "You should rest, and eat some more." He had eaten only broth and bread for her. "Where are you going?" Rowan seldom showed such exasperation.

Rook shrugged. He was only going to his father's hut to get clothing and coverings. A jerkin for when the night air grew chill on his shoulders. Maybe some leggings, and sheepskins to sleep on. And he wanted the pigskin shoes his father had made for him. He was tired of banging his bare feet on stones.

But he did not know how it was that he had started to feel the cold and the stones again, and he did not know how to say any of this to Rowan.

"Oh, toads take you, go wherever you want." Rowan turned her face away.

Rook stood a moment longer, but could not think how to help her. Silently he went away, walking off between the hazel bushes that edged Robin's clearing, striding uphill into oak forest.

It should have been a fine day. Sunny, warm. Runkling trotted along cheerily, grunting with mindless good humor. Dogs, too, were like that, happy for no reason. That dog Father used to have, the one that helped herd the pigs, even after the foresters had cut its toes off, it still wagged its tail, happy just to be patted, fed, be with its family.

Stupid.

Or—maybe brave?

Rook slipped like a breeze along the ravine where he had found Tod in the man trap. The stream still dashed along like black squirrels leaping, cold and swift, singing its wild song. Rook still thought there ought to be grayling in the riffles. But it all looked different to him somehow, and not just because the sun was shining today. Something had changed.

"Come on, Runkling." He spoke gently to the little pig as he led it through the thinning outskirts of the forest, trotting through straggling woods, then between groves amid stony meadowland growing thick with furze and wild mint and pignut and a hundred other plants—the sort of place where Rowan might go to hunt for herbs.

Again, the meadows looked different somehow.

Beautiful. Cowslips in bloom. And there, ahead, the hut, with the fallen blossoms of the crab-apple tree lying on its stones like a fragrant white blessing.

"That's the house my father built, Runkling," he whispered to the little pig, and he stood just looking for a moment before he knelt and crawled down into the shelter his father had left behind, snug in wintertime, but dim and cool now in the summer heat.

His hand touched something warm, solid and alive. Someone's shoulder.

Rook gasped. For just an eyeblink instant he thought it was his father lying there sleeping. Then the person awoke with a whimper and jerked upright, edging away from him.

Peering in the dim light, Rook whispered, "Tod?"

Tod turned his face toward the wall. "Go away."

Rook said, gently enough, "What, I am supposed to walk off and leave you in the man trap now?"

Tod did not answer except by stiffening and shrinking against the wall.

Rook stared, thinking of Rowan so shadowed today, and now Tod even worse, and he still didn't know what to do to help.

He heard quick movements nearby, and a snuffling sound. Runkling, rooting around inside the hut, exploring. Rook reached over, lifted the little pig and placed him in Tod's lap. He did not let go until Tod responded. It took a moment, but at last Tod's arms stirred, lifted Runkling and hugged him. Tod's chest heaved. A sob, a sigh? Rook considered that he did not need to know. He started hunting along the walls of the hut for the things he had come to fetch.

He found an old jerkin and slipped it on. It was a bit tight, but he could still wear it. Sitting on the dirt floor, he put on the sheepskin wrappings to protect his legs from thorns. And the shoes, stiff and dry now, neglected for almost two years, but he eased them on anyway. They would soften as he wore them.

He gathered everything that was left: bedding, an old mantle, spare jerkins and leggings, flint and steel. He wrapped it all in a blanket and pushed it out of the entryway ahead of him. Then he looked over his shoulder at Tod and said, "Come on."

Tod did not move except to shake his head.

"You can't just stay here," Rook said.

"Why not?"

"How will you live?"

"I don't want to live."

Rook turned to peer at him, crouching. After a while he said, "You can't just give up."

"Why not?"

"You can't. You have to go on."

"Is that what you did?"

Silence.

Finally Rook said, "That's what I'm doing now."

"So go ahead. Go away. Leave me alone."

Rook shook his head, reached for Tod's hand and grasped it. "Come on." He tugged. "Robin Hood is searching for you."

For a long moment the name hung like a woodland spirit, a power, in the cool shadowy air of the hut. Then Tod sighed and moved. He put Runkling down and reached for his crutch. He crawled out of the hut after Rook. He stood and slowly followed Rook into the forest.

It took Rook and Tod until twilight to find Robin. All afternoon Tod limped along with his crutch, and Rook plodded beside him, until at last they reached Robin Hood's camp—and then Robin was not there. One of the outlaws, Will Scathelock, led them to him.

He led them into a secret place such as Rook had never seen before, or even dreamed of. Made by the ancient green power of the Lady, it must have been, so perfect a ring of silver linden trees around an open space bigger than Fountain Dale, yet only velvety grass grew there. Protected by the *aelfe,* it must have been, so that no henchmen of king or lord would find it, no forest wanderers would stumble upon it, so that only those who grieved could go there.

This was the place where they buried the dead. Near the center of the green circle rimmed by silver trees, a rectangle of raw earth showed where Robin Hood and Little John had laid the dead outlaw. They were just finishing their work there, mounding the grave.

Will Scathelock signaled by giving the twitter of a wagtail bird as they entered, and Robin turned to see who it was.

"Tod, lad!" Robin let his spade fall with a clatter, almost running to meet them. Tod gave an odd sort of choked sound and lurched toward Robin, dropping his crutch. Falling to his knees in the grass, Robin caught him and gathered him into his arms. Tod hugged Robin's neck and wept.

"Tod, my poor lad." Robin stroked the boy's heaving back as Tod cried like a baby on his shoulder. Rook heard Tod sobbing. He saw how Robin's blue eyes had gone brighter than ever with tears. He heard his own breath coming in uncouth gasps and felt the salty wetness on his own face.

He was crying.

But Rook made no effort to stop his weeping or hide his tears or wipe them from his face. Even a wolf might cry sometimes. But, truth to tell, he wasn't a wolf or a creature of the wild or a wild boy either. He was just Rook, the swineherd's son, and he would cry when sorrow touched his heart.

Fourteen

S ee the stone? This is the place," Robin Hood told Rook, passing his hand like a sailing hawk over a span of greensward near the center of the linden circle.

Close beside Robin stood Rowan, and his other hand hugged her shoulders as if he still feared he might lose her, his daughter.

Rowan seemed to be scanning the ring of silver-leafed trees. Now that a few days had passed and everyone was healing, so was she. Tykell had returned to her. She had slept. Her grave face was peaceful, visionary. "The *aelfe*," she murmured, gazing. "They're here. Do you see them, Rook?"

He looked at her without bothering to shake his head. She knew he had never been able to see the *aelfe*.

"Where?" Robin asked.

"Between the lindens, faintly, like moonlight that has lingered in the daytime."

Robin nodded. Rook looked between the trees ringing the glade, and somehow this time he did see something, a shimmer, a stirring as if earth and forest were breathing. He couldn't glimpse the wise, ancient faces of the *aelfe*, but it didn't matter. He could sense their protection. Their presence would keep anyone of cowardly or evil heart out of this place.

The king's foresters, for instance. They or bounty hunters would never trouble these graves. Or the Sheriff of Nottingham.

But the Sheriff's son could enter here. Tod was neither cowardly nor evil of heart, and here he came now, limping into the glade, steadying himself with a staff instead of his crutch, stronger than he'd been a week before but still a bit slower than the others. He cast a wondering glance around him, but if he felt the presence of the spirits, he did not fear them.

Rook gave him a nod of greeting.

"Is that it?" Tod asked. "Is that the marker?" He pointed his chin toward it—just a flat forest stone much like any of the others that dotted the linden grove.

Rook looked to Robin Hood. "This is where my father lies?"

"Yes. That is Jack Woodsby's stone. I promise you."

And where better could he lie than within the silver ring of this holy grove.

Rook swallowed, nodded, and knelt, with Runkling snuffling and grunting by his side. Runkling did not root or slobber at the soft grass. Even the animals seemed to know this was a sacred place. Tykell sat like a wolf-dog statue at Rowan's feet, as if he had forgotten for the time being how badly he wanted to eat Runkling.

Kneeling, Rook clutched the bundle of flowers he had carried here, wild roses and day's-eye and key-of-heaven flowers, the sweetest that earth had to offer. Rook felt very much his father's son with a forest breeze ruffling his shorn hair, with his jerkin and leggings and the pigskin shoes, well oiled now, soft on his feet. One by one he scattered the flowers. For a moment he knelt amid their sweetness to remember his father's gentle face and kind hands.

Then he stood, drifting in the moment like a trout in a deep river pool, just being. Clouds stirred ever so slightly in the sky. The *aelfe* hovered like silver mist.

Somewhere a robin rejoiced. Somewhere a dove mourned.

Tod spoke. "Rook," he asked in a voice much softer than his usual piping tones, "did your father beat you?"

"No." Jack Swineherd had seldom so much as raised his voice in anger. Remembering, Rook felt his voice go soft. "He wasn't like that."

Tod nodded and turned his face upward to the tall man beside him. "Robin, did you have a father?"

"Of course, Tod." Robin's tone crinkled with a glint of his usual merriment.

"Did he beat you?"

"No, lad." No merriment now.

"Was he—your father—did he—if you got lost, would he want you back?"

"Yes, lad." Rook had never heard Robin's voice so gentle, so sad.

Tod stood silent for a moment, then asked one last question. "Is he—Robin, is your father yet alive?"

"No, he's long dead, Tod." Hugging Rowan even closer to his side, Robin put his other arm around the Sheriff's son. Yet his blue-eyed gaze met Rook's eyes as if he were speaking to Rook alone. "He's dead and gone. But he lives on in my heart."

Holding Runkling, Rook rubbed noses with the piglet, then offered it with outstretched hands to Tod. "Take him with you."

On horseback, sheltered by the last great oak at the eastern edge of Sherwood Forest, Tod gazed out over open, rolling hills. But he shifted his gaze to gawk at Rook. "Take Runkling? But he's yours!"

"Take him." Rook laid Runkling on the saddle in front of Tod.

"I can't!" Still, Tod couldn't keep from clutching at the little pig, lifting Runkling into a one-armed hug. With his other hand he kept tight rein on the hot-blooded horse Robin's merry men had stolen from Nottingham's stables for him. It had been two full moons since Tod had hurt himself. He needed no splint on his leg anymore, and he could walk without a staff, but he could not have walked the journey that lay before him, a distance of many leagues. He had accepted the horse gladly.

Even more gladly he held Runkling to his shoulder, although he told Rook, "You can't give him to me."

"No? But methinks I can. Take him."

From the back of the tall charger, Tod gazed down at Rook. "You're smiling," he said, his tone soft with wonder. "I don't think I've ever seen you smile before."

"I'm glad to be rid of you," Rook lied, teasing.

"Really? Well, then, I'll be sure to come back someday. To annoy you."

"Do that," Rook said.

From the forest shadows another voice spoke. "You be sure you do come back, Tod, lad." Robin Hood stepped into view and lifted his bow to Tod in a gesture that was half blessing, half an outlaw's defiance of all that made life hard. "Our best thoughts go with you."

"Thank you," Tod whispered, and Rook could see the tears glimmering in his eyes. "Thank you all." Hugging Runkling, Tod wheeled his horse and sent it cantering away from the forest.

From the shelter of the oak, Rook and Robin watched after him until he disappeared over a barley-covered hilltop.

Then Robin studied Rook with a soft glance. "Now, why did you give him Runkling, for the love of the Lady?"

Rook stood silent, gazing into blue distance.

"You wish you could go with him," Robin said.

Rook nodded. "He ought to have someone with him," he said, his voice gruff again. "But he thinks he can ride all that way by himself. . . ."

"He will be all right," Robin said. "He's well provisioned. And Tod is a proper young fox, remember?"

Rook nodded, remembering how he had hated Tod the day Robin had first called the boy a young fox. But much had happened since. The sunshine looked more golden to Rook now, the streams clearer, the fish fairer, even the oaks more green. Something had changed.

In me.

"Look." Rook pointed to where dust rose beyond the hilltop. Already Tod was well on his way.

Robin nodded. "So far, so fine."

Tod was riding toward the holdings of his mother's people, several days to the east. And if they tried to send him back to his father, he would ride on to the king's court in London. Perhaps the king would give him refuge for the sake of the Nottingham name.

"It's what he has to do," Robin said, maybe to still his own doubts and fears. "He can't just stay here. He's too young to be branded a wolf's head."

"No younger than I," Rook grumbled.

Robin glanced at him with crinkling, twinkling blue eyes. "Rook, you will always be older than Tod. You're nearly your father's age already."

Let Robin tease all he liked. At the thought of his father, Rook smiled.